KV-677-844

James Pattinson is a full-time author who, despite having travelled throughout the world, still lives in the remote village where he grew up. He has written magazine articles, short stories and radio features as well as numerous novels.

O Callaghan

THE WILD ONE

Hector Langdon volunteered for the army in World War I when he was no more than seventeen years old, though he gave his age as twenty. It was the kind of reckless action he was to take all his life, much to the regret of his solicitor father, who wished him to follow in the same profession. That would have been far too boring for Hector's taste, so he drifted from one occupation to another after the war. It seemed he had to be forever on the move — until he met Eva Gray. And even that meeting was to lead to tragedy.

Books by James Pattinson
Published by The House of Ulverscroft:

WILD JUSTICE
THE WHEEL OF FORTUNE
ACROSS THE NARROW SEAS
CONTACT MR. DELGADO
LADY FROM ARGENTINA
SOLDIER, SAIL NORTH
THE TELEPHONE MURDERS
SQUEAKY CLEAN
A WIND ON THE HEATH
ONE-WAY TICKET
AWAY WITH MURDER
LAST IN CONVOY
THE ANTWERP APPOINTMENT
THE HONEYMOON CAPER
STEEL
THE DEADLY SHORE
THE MURMANSK ASSIGNMENT
FLIGHT TO THE SEA
DEATH OF A GO-BETWEEN
DANGEROUS ENCHANTMENT
THE PETRONOV PLAN
THE SPOILERS
HOMECOMING
SOME JOB
BAVARIAN SUNSET
THE LIBERATORS
STRIDE
FINAL RUN

JAMES PATTINSON

---◆---

THE WILD ONE

Complete and Unabridged

ULVERSCROFT
Leicester

First published in Great Britain in 1999 by
Robert Hale Limited
London

First Large Print Edition
published 2001
by arrangement with
Robert Hale Limited
London

British Library CIP Data

Pattinson, James
   The wild one.—Large print ed.—
   Ulverscroft large print series: adventure & suspense
   1. Large type books
   I. Title
   823.9'14 [F]

   ISBN 0–7089–4424–8

Published by
F. A. Thorpe (Publishing)
Anstey, Leicestershire

Set by Words & Graphics Ltd.
Anstey, Leicestershire
Printed and bound in Great Britain by
T. J. International Ltd., Padstow, Cornwall

This book is printed on acid-free paper

1

All Over

Martin Gray was certain he would never forget the day when his uncle, Hector Langdon, was hanged by the neck until dead. Well, it was not the kind of thing you could easily banish from your memory, was it? And it would have been especially difficult for a boy of twelve, for whom Uncle Hector had been something of a hero.

It was a day in November, the year 1929; a miserable day in all respects; the weather damp and chilly, no sun to be seen and fog hanging over the fields like a dripping blanket. The family was gathered in the drawing-room, where a fire seemed to have caught the general mood of depression and refused adamantly to do anything more than send a thin wisp of smoke up the chimney. There were three of them present besides Martin: Edward and Mary Gray, his parents, and his Aunt Eva.

The drawing-room was not large — none of the rooms in Mill House were — and normally it was used only on Sundays and special occasions like Christmas Day. This day qualified as a special occasion, though it was certainly not one for any celebration, and no one in that little group appeared to be enjoying it; they were for the most part silent and seemed to avoid meeting one another's eyes. When Mr Gray rather noisily cleared his throat the others glanced at him as if he had broken some kind of taboo.

'That wretched fire,' he said. 'Can't think why it won't get up. Must be the coal.'

He spoke testily, as if the refusal of the coal to burst into flame were a deliberate act of misbehaviour designed to cause inconvenience to all concerned.

He was a tall, rather skinny man in his late thirties, with limp brown hair receding from the temples; not really handsome but not bad-looking either. He had served in the 4th Norfolks in the Great War and had been wounded in the arm and the leg in the First Battle of Gaza. He still felt some discomfort from the wounds, especially on days like this when the weather was raw.

Now he got up suddenly from his chair, seized the poker from where it was lying in the brass fender and started attacking the lumps of coal as though he had a grudge against them. The only result of this operation was an increase in the volume of smoke, some of which came out into the room, polluting the air but not making it any warmer.

'For goodness' sake, Ted!' Mrs Gray said. 'Do stop it. You're only making matters worse.'

'Oh, very well,' he said pettishly, throwing the poker down into the fender to join the shovel and the tongs and the brush with a clatter that was almost as disturbing as a dropped collection plate in church.

He returned to his chair, sat down and pulled a watch from his pocket. He compared this with the clock on the mantelpiece, appeared satisfied that both were registering the same time and put it away again.

The clock had a gilt face and black hands. The black marble case was in the shape of a Grecian temple with miniature fluted pillars supporting the roof on each side. In the silence that followed the attack on the coal the ticking of the clock could be clearly heard; and it occurred to Martin that it was ticking away Uncle Hector's life, second by second. He wanted to stop it, but what good would that have done? You could not stop time.

There were two armchairs in the room and a chesterfield with loose covers. His mother and Aunt Eva were sitting on the sofa, while his father and he had the chairs. Now and then he would shift his position on the chair because it was not very comfortable, but whenever he fidgeted his mother would give him a severe look and a shake of the head.

In one corner of the room was an aspidistra in a brass container perched on a tall stand, and in another corner was an oil lamp, also on a stand but this one of brass. The lamp, at present unlit, had a large tasselled shade, from the top of which the glass chimney protruded like the upper part of a tumbler. The wallpaper did nothing to lift the spirits; it was predominantly dull brown in colour, varied here and there by some birds of an unidentifiable species on the wing to some destination known only to themselves.

Martin glanced furtively at Aunt Eva to see how she was bearing up in the painful circumstances. Her face was expressionless, but he could see that her hands were clasped tightly in her lap, and he guessed that she was making a great effort to keep her emotions under control. It must have been very difficult for her.

She was his father's sister, but several years younger than her brother. Martin thought she was very beautiful. She was his favourite aunt, and be believed he was in love with her. He was in love with quite a number of film actresses too, but of course he had never got any nearer to them than a seat in a cinema, and then they were nothing more than images on the silver screen, while Aunt Eva was real flesh and blood.

She had fluffy golden hair in a mass of small natural curls, light blue eyes and a sweet little nose with a slight tilt at the end. She had a small mouth with Cupid's-bow lips and teeth that were perhaps just a shade too prominent for absolute perfection. She was petite, with a boyish figure that was just right for the fashions of the time. She could easily have passed for twenty, though in fact she was closer to thirty and had a daughter aged six.

The daughter's name was Crystal, and she was being kept well out of the way until the dreadful business was finished with. For the present she was staying with her paternal grandparents in Norwich, and it was hoped to keep her ignorant of just what had happened until she was old enough to be more capable of handling the revelation. Whether that was at all possible was extremely doubtful, but they could but try.

Martin had recently read a poem by Oscar Wilde called 'The Ballad of Reading Gaol', and in the circumstances it had made a deep impression on him. Now a particular line came into his head: 'The hangman with his gardener's gloves . . . ' He wondered whether hangmen really did wear gardener's gloves, and if so, why? Would they not have made it awkward to handle the rope and make the knot? But perhaps the knot had already been made, and all that needed to be done was to slip the noose over the prisoner's head and draw it tight round his neck. They put a hood over the head too, didn't they? Was that before or after adjusting the noose?

Then he remembered some more of the poem, a whole verse. It went round and round in his head.

It is sweet to dance to violins
When Love and Life are fair:
To dance to flutes, to dance to lutes
Is delicate and rare:
But it is not sweet with nimble feet
To dance upon the air!

He had a vision of Uncle Hector dangling at the end of a rope and his feet jerking up and down. How long did it take for a man to die from hanging? Did he feel much pain? Did anybody really know for certain? How could they?

When the clock began to strike it came as a shock to all of them, though they had been expecting it, waiting for it. Eva gave a little startled cry and Mr Gray took his watch out again, just to make a check on the timing. When the last stroke of the clock had sounded he put the watch back in his pocket with an air of finality and said:

'Well that's it. It's all over now. All over.'

Eva began to sob. She was shivering, perhaps not from cold, though there was certainly a chill in the room, with that sulky fire giving out so little heat. Mary Gray put an arm round the woman who was now a widow, making an effort to comfort her. She had never cared much for this sister-in-law, whom she felt to be in part at least to blame for the tragedy that had occurred; but at this moment she had only sympathy for her.

Martin stood up suddenly, gave a choking cry and ran from the room. He could not stay with the others. He had to be alone with his grief and his regret.

2

Veteran

Hector Langdon, it had to be admitted, had always been something of a scamp. He was also a charmer. Men and women alike fell under his spell; they might know only too well what kind of a man he was, but it made no difference; they could not help themselves. Not everyone, of course. There were some, chiefly men, who hated his guts, and perhaps had reason to; but they were in the minority. Mostly he was welcomed wherever he went.

His father was a solicitor, and it had been expected that he, the Langdons' only child, would in course of time take his place in the family firm. It soon became apparent, however, that as the boy grew older he had no inclination to taking up the legal profession as a career. Not that he seemed to be attracted to any other profession or trade either. At school he might have done better if he had been prepared to apply himself with more diligence to his studies, for he was certainly not without ability. But it was on the playing-field and not in the classroom that he made his mark. He was popular with his peers but something of a bane to his masters.

He was still at school in 1914 when war broke out in Europe, and like many boys of his age he could hardly wait to get into uniform. He was just seventeen when he enlisted, giving his age as twenty. His parents were horrified when he told them; but there was nothing they could do about it; the die was cast. He had a brief period of training and then was shipped across the Channel to the killing fields of France.

He endured three years of hell in the trenches and emerged without a scratch and with the rank of sergeant. He had always had luck; maybe it was something that went with the wildness. He had a decoration too: the military medal. It had been awarded for bravery under fire when he had gone into no-man's-land to bring in a wounded comrade from a shell-hole. He always made light of it, saying it was the sort of thing you did without thinking. But there could be no doubt that he was really rather proud of it.

Arthur and Frances Langdon now hoped that he would settle down and study for the law, as it had always been their hope that he would. But there was never any likelihood of that. He wanted something more interesting, exciting even. And what was there interesting or exciting in a provincial solicitor's office where the business was mainly concerned with wills and deeds and petty lawsuits regarding property, disputes between neighbours over a few feet of worthless ground and that kind of thing? Nothing ever came the way of Langdon and Thorpe that would have made headlines in the national press; it was all routine stuff, horribly dull and uninteresting. That at any rate was Hector Langdon's opinion, and he wanted none of it.

'So what do you intend to do?' his father asked.

And the fact was that he was somewhat in awe of this son who, at the age of little more than twenty, was a hardened veteran of the most terrible war that had ever been fought; a war in which carnage of hitherto inconceivable proportions had taken place in the mud and horror of those trenches not so many miles and yet a world away. He himself could only imagine what it must have been like to live through that nightmare. Hector could have told him if he had wished, but he did not wish to; he refused to talk about it. And Arthur Langdon did not press him to do so; he felt it might have been too harrowing for both of them. So all he knew was that his son had gone away a boy and had returned a man; a man with whom he felt it almost impossible to communicate on level terms.

Again he asked: 'What do you intend to do?'

'I haven't decided yet.'

'But you must do something.'

'I realize that.'

'And you are still unwilling to join the firm?'

'Yes.'

'Well, I am sorry about that, truly sorry. I had hoped — '

Arthur Langdon, a dapper little man with a neatly trimmed moustache and beard now speckled with grey, was totally unlike his son in almost every respect, physically as well as mentally. He was by nature a cautious man who invariably looked before he leaped, never took any avoidable risk and was extremely guarded when advising clients. He could only suppose that Hector had inherited his spirit of recklessness from his mother, who had on occasion been known to act in an unconventional way. But with her he had usually been able to exert a restraining influence and put a curb on any possible extravagances. With Hector, from a very early age, he had had no such success, and he had been driven to the unpalatable conclusion that the boy was simply ungovernable; at least by him.

So, when he came to think about it, would

it have been such a wise move to bring this young man, this untamed spirit, into the staid old firm of Langdon and Thorpe? Would it not have been too great a risk even to contemplate? The thought of what havoc might be caused by Hector's entry into the somewhat rarefied atmosphere of the solicitors' office sent a shiver down his spine. He would never fit in and he could never be groomed to an acceptable standard of behaviour for such a profession. It would not have been simply a question of smoothing away a few rough edges; what would have been required was a complete transformation of character. And that was something neither he nor anyone else could have hoped to accomplish.

Hector might have been reading his thoughts. He said: 'It wouldn't work, Dad. You know that, don't you? I'm not cut out for it; never will be.'

'So what are you cut out for?'

The question was put rather testily, and Hector had to admit to himself that his father had some reason to be testy. He had been a disappointment to the old boy in almost every possible way. Arthur Langdon had perhaps hoped for a son in the same mould as himself; if so he had been sadly frustrated. And there had been no other child, male or female, to make his dreams come true.

'I don't know,' Hector said. 'I'll have to take a look around. No need to hurry, is there?'

'Well, perhaps not. But don't leave it too long. I can foresee difficult times ahead, and I'll not be happy until I see you in a decent job with an assured future.'

Hector controlled an inclination to laugh. He knew the kind of job his father was referring to: insurance company, bank, estate agency, that sort of thing. Start at the bottom and work your way up the ladder; retire on a pension after half a lifetime of monotonous drudgery. It was not for him and never would be. He had other ideas for his future, though it had to be admitted that they were all pretty hazy for the moment.

'Things will work out,' he said. 'Don't worry.'

3

Instinct

He met Harry Wentworth in a public house in Norwich. Wentworth was also an ex-service man. He had been in the Royal Flying Corps and had come out with the rank of captain and a broken nose sustained when making a crash-landing in a field of beet. He had red hair and freckles and a carefree outlook on life. Hector recognized a man after his own heart and took to him at once.

Wentworth had recently bought a small-holding some five miles out of the city. It was a pretty run-down sort of place and the few acres of land that went with it consisted mainly of rough pasture. He told Hector that he had no intention of farming it; that was just not in his line. What he proposed was to set up a riding school. He had had some experience with horses and knew what was what in that line. He believed there was money to be made in teaching people to ride for pleasure, and as the place was within easy reach of the city it was unlikely to suffer from lack of custom.

14

'Why don't you come and take a look at the layout? That's if you have nothing better to do.'

Hector had nothing better to do, and it was still early in the day, so he readily agreed to the proposal.

Wentworth had a car, which was parked in the inn yard. It was a nine horsepower Rover, an open two-seater painted a garish red, which seemed to go well with its owner. He started it with the handle and they got in.

'Temperamental little beast,' Wentworth said. 'Always breaking down in the most inconvenient places. Get something better when the business really takes off.'

He seemed absolutely confident that this time would very soon come, and Hector could not help being infected by his enthusiasm. Horses had never figured much in his life. He had seen the poor brutes dragging guns in France and he had seen officers riding them, but he himself had had nothing to do with anything equestrian. Now, however, with Harry Wentworth enthusing volubly over the unrivalled merits of the noble animal he began, even before reaching the proposed riding establishment, to reflect that perhaps he had been missing something wholly desirable.

Chestnuts, as the place was called, though

so close to the boundaries of the city, might well have been deep in the heart of the countryside. It was down a rutted lane with tall hedges on each side, and at the entrance were the two chestnut trees from which it took its name.

'Well, here we are,' Wentworth said. 'This is it.'

Apart from the trees, which were quite majestic, Hector felt that there was nothing very impressive about the place. The house was red brick, much weathered, somewhat dilapidated and in need of paint. It had a pantiled roof and there was a lean-to at one end which was probably used as a washhouse. At the rear was a large yard into which Wentworth drove the car and stopped it.

'Right then,' he said. 'Let's go and take a look.'

There were more outbuildings than Hector would have expected, though all were in the same neglected condition as the house. Wentworth seemed to feel a need to explain.

'Used to belong to an old man whose wife died some years ago. He'd been living on his own and just letting things slide. Then he died too and the place came up for sale — cheap because of the state it was in. I saw its potential and got a bargain. Some of those sheds can easily be converted into stables.

And there's the barn too, which will be handy for storage purposes; fodder and so on.'

The barn was of clay-lump construction. Wentworth led the way to it, and Hector could see places where the tarred coating of plaster had fallen away from the walls and the exposed clay was being eroded by rainwater. The tall wooden doors were rotting at the bottom and were hanging askew. Inside along one wall were horse stalls with mangers and tethers. Above was a hay loft.

'You see,' Wentworth said. 'Everything is here. Just needs a spot of renovation and we're on our way.'

Hector wondered whether the 'we' was a slip of the tongue. It almost seemed as if the man were including him in the scheme.

In a paddock were two horses, the total extent for the time being of Wentworth's livestock.

'Need more, of course. Half a dozen at least. Couldn't really make a go of it with less.'

'So you're planning to buy some more?'

'Now there,' Wentworth said, 'we come up against the problem.'

'Problem?'

'Cash flow, old boy. Fact is, I've run out of the ready. It's so damned frustrating, I can tell you. Here I am, sitting on a potential goldmine, and just because I'm short of a few quid I can't start digging the stuff out. You see how it is?'

Hector did see, and he sympathized with Wentworth. In a similar situation he himself would have felt the same way.

'Have you thought of raising a loan?'

Wentworth gave a rueful laugh. 'Have I not! Went to my bank manager. Put it to him. Golden opportunity. Not to be missed. Chance of a lifetime and all that. He didn't see it. Tried the old soldier line. Returning hero. Done my bit for my country, not to mention the jolly old monarch. That sort of thing. Cut no ice with him. Man's got a heart of stone. Said he didn't feel justified in risking the bank's money on such a venture. No vision of course; none at all.'

'How much were you asking for?'

'A thousand.'

'Um! It's a lot of money.'

'Just pump-priming. Bread cast on the waters.'

'Have you tried anywhere else?'

'Moneylenders? I'm steering clear of them. Sharks. No, I'm afraid there's only one thing for it. I'll have to find a partner with a spot of the necessary.'

'Anyone in mind?'

'Oh, I know two or three who'd jump at

the chance. Trouble is, none of them's the sort I'd like to work with.'

Hector agreed that this was a snag. A partner had to be someone after your own heart.

They went into the house. The interior was much like the exterior: in need of renovation. The bits and pieces of furniture looked as though they had been picked up in saleyards. Hector, with his recent experience of far worse quarters, was not repelled by what he saw. Wentworth produced a half-full bottle of whisky and a couple of glasses, and they sat in the kitchen, drinking and talking. At the end of an hour Hector brought out the suggestion that had been revolving in his mind ever since his host had revealed his problem.

'How would you like me for a partner?'

'You?' Wentworth said, as though such an idea had never until that moment entered his head.

'Yes, me.'

'Are you serious?'

'Of course I am.'

He was also a trifle inebriated, partly by the whisky and partly by the prospect of joining Harry Wentworth in a venture that so strongly appealed to him. His only fear at that moment was that the man might reject him.

'Don't you think I'd make a suitable partner?'

Wentworth drank some more whisky and seemed to be thinking it over, while Hector watched him with some anxiety, since now that he had made the suggestion he felt that there was nothing he desired more than to throw in his lot with the ex-flyer.

Finally Wentworth said: 'Well, it's pretty short acquaintance and I know very little about you, but the fact is, I like you. Some people might say it's a rash decision, but that's me, that's old Harry W. Act on instinct. It's never let me down. Well, not often.'

'So it's a go?'

'It's a go. That's if you've got the thousand quid. Have you?'

'Not at the moment. But I'm pretty sure I can get it.'

'Fine. But don't hang about. The sooner we get this thing up and running, the sooner we'll be raking in the profits.'

'I'll drink to that,' Hector said.

And he did so.

4

No Documents

'A thousand pounds!' Arthur Langdon looked both shocked and incredulous.

'Is this some kind of joke?'

'Not at all,' Hector said.

'But you can't be serious.'

'Never more so.'

This interview was taking place in Mr Langdon's study-cum-library in the solid Edwardian house which had been the family home ever since he had bought it when Hector was six years old. It was a bigger place than they really needed, and Hector had always found it rather gloomy and depressing. He still had this same impression of it when he returned from France, and he felt that one thing he had to do as soon as possible was to get away from it.

'So you're asking me to lend you a thousand to throw away on some hare-brained scheme that this fellow Wentworth has thought up?'

'It's not a hare-brained scheme. It's a

perfectly sound and well thought out enterprise.'

'A riding school! What do you know about horses?'

'Nothing at present. But Wentworth does. I'll soon learn.'

'So you'll be the first pupil in your own school.' Langdon spoke sarcastically. 'A fine start, I must say. How long have you known this man?'

'Not long,' Hector said. He felt it would hardly strengthen his case if he admitted that he had met Wentworth for the first time earlier that very day. 'But he's the genuine article. Was a captain in the Flying Corps.'

This information appeared to make very little in the way of a favourable impression on Arthur Langdon. Any possible ability to shoot enemy aircraft out of the skies was hardly a qualification for running a successful riding school.

'Where is this place of his?'

Hector told him. 'There's a house and stabling as well as plenty of pasture. It's very suitable.'

'And it's his? Not rented?'

'Oh yes. He's the owner.'

'What sort of condition is it in?'

'Not bad.'

'Which of course means it's not good

either. A ruin of a place with no end of work needing to be done on it, I have no doubt. That's why he's looking for a partner with a thousand pounds to sink in it. Well, my lad, I'll tell you straight, he's not having any of my money. Not a penny. So you can get that idea out of your head straight-away.'

Hector was disappointed but not too cast down by this rebuff, since he had had no great expectation that his father would cough up the necessary cash. He was too careful with money to hand out what was quite a considerable sum on a venture in which he had no confidence whatever. No doubt he had grave suspicions regarding the bona fides of this Harry Wentworth, whom he had never met; and Hector felt it was hardly likely that these suspicions would have been at all allayed if he had made the acquaintance of the man. The very qualities in Wentworth which had such an appeal to Hector were the sort that would have been well calculated to alienate his father.

So Arthur Langdon as a possible source of capital for the equestrian project could be ruled out of the reckoning. He was a non-starter; that fact had to be accepted.

But Hector had a second string to his bow; and if one was useless he felt that the other might well prove to be far more serviceable.

In giving herself to Arthur Langdon, Frances Brett, as she then was, had not come empty-handed. Indeed, she possessed in her own right a small fortune of several thousand pounds that had been left to her in the will of a bachelor great-uncle whose favourite she was. Arthur would very much have liked to gain possession of this money, but he had never been able to do so, though he had argued persuasively that in his hands it would be invested to the very best advantage, since he knew a thing or two about such matters. Frances admitted that he probably did know a great deal more about financial dealings than she did, but she saw no reason why the money had to be in his hands in order to bring in a satisfactory return, seeing that she could follow his advice in the management of it without necessarily handing over the entire capital sum to him. It was her money and she intended that it should remain under her control.

This was when Arthur Langdon discovered that his wife had a will of her own and that in his dealings with her he could not always count on getting his own way. So the legacy remained in her hands and, invested to the best advantage, provided quite a decent regular income. Which was a most satisfactory state of affairs for the lady, since it meant that she had no need to take the begging-bowl to her husband whenever she needed extra spending money.

Knowing this, and having drawn a blank with his father, Hector took his request for a loan of one thousand pounds to the other and more impressionable parent. He felt sure that with her he would have more success. It would not be the first time he had gone to her with a request for money, and he had never known her to refuse; he had such a charming and persuasive way with him, and she, though not blind to the many blemishes in his character, loved him very deeply nonetheless.

So when he had painted for her in glowing colours the plan of going into partnership with a man named Harry Wentworth in a riding school she did not immediately pour scorn on the whole idea as Arthur had. She merely said:

'Are you quite sure this is what you want to do, dear?'

'Oh, absolutely.'

'You haven't known this Captain Wentworth very long, have you?'

'Long enough. With some people you just know.'

'Yes, I suppose you do.'

Frances Langdon was no fool, and she had no more confidence in the future of the Chestnuts riding school than her husband had. She knew quite well that, though Hector might refer to the thousand pounds as a loan, there would be little chance of its ever being repaid. It would in effect be a gift. But this did not deter her.

And was there not just a faint possibility that the riding school would prove a success? Miracles did happen. And if not, it would at least be an experience from which Hector might learn something. Besides which, did he not deserve some reward for those years of his youth spent in the hell of the battlefield? She believed he did.

'Very well,' she said. 'I will let you have the money.'

Hector gave her a hug and a kiss. 'You're a brick, Mother. You're one in a million.'

'I'm also probably very stupid,' she said. 'Your father will certainly say so.'

She was right about that. He did not use those precise words, but she was left in no doubt that in his opinion she had acted very unwisely indeed.

'It's throwing money away. You'll never see

a penny of it back.'

She did not tell him that she was of the same opinion on that point. And that she did not care.

'It's what he wants to do,' she said. 'I think he should be given his head. Just for this once anyway.'

Arthur Langdon snorted. 'And a fine mess he'll make of it, we can be sure. Well, it's out of my hands now.'

Nevertheless, he made an attempt to retain some control of the situation by suggesting to Hector that he should be allowed to examine the documents pertaining to the partnership agreement before anything was signed. He was aghast to learn from his son when he broached the matter that there would be nothing whatever to sign. It was to be a gentlemen's agreement; a handshake was all that was necessary.

Arthur Langdon stared at his son in utter disbelief. 'Are you completely mad?'

'I don't think so.'

'And yet you are proposing to sink one thousand pounds in a partnership which will be no more binding than a rubber band?'

'It'll be all right. You worry too much.'

'With you for a son I have a lot to worry about. When will you start to act like a sensible human being?'

'Like you, for instance?'

This question seemed to embarrass the older man. 'Well — '

Hector grinned. 'The answer is never. I'm just not made that way. Sorry, Dad, but that's how it is, and you've got to accept me as I am because I'll never change.'

'And you still intend to make this contract with nothing more than a handshake to make it stick?'

'That's about it.'

Arthur Langdon made a despairing gesture with his hands, sighed deeply and said: 'Well, have it your own way. I've given my advice, but if you won't take it you won't. I simply do not understand.'

'No, you don't, do you?' Hector said. 'And I'm afraid you never will.'

And then he went on to hint, without saying it in just so many words, that there was some kind of mystical rapport between men who had taken a hand in that recent great conflict of arms which could never be understood by any mere civilian who had done nothing more than keep the home fires burning till the boys came home. There were so many who had come back from the trenches as virtual strangers to those whom they had left behind when they marched off to war.

So all he could do was repeat what he had said before: 'It'll be all right.'

He wondered whether it would. But the question did not bother him.

5

Happy Days

The spring of 1919 was the first since the Great War had ended with the signing of the Armistice on November the Eleventh 1918. The Kaiser was now in Holland chopping wood, the Bolsheviks were in the ascendant in Russia, the German economy was in ruins and the Chestnuts Riding School was just getting into its stride.

Hector had gone to live with Harry Wentworth in the farmhouse, much to his mother's distress, and he had bought a second-hand Douglas motor-cycle. He had also learned to ride a horse and enjoyed it.

There were now three horses and four ponies occupying the stables on which some essential work had been carried out by a local builder. The house had also received some attention, but it was still in a rather dilapidated condition. A woman came in daily to do the chores and a bit of plain cooking. Her name was Mrs Ludkin, a plump, cheerful, middle-aged person, whose husband was a farm labourer.

There were two regular employees now. One was a wizened little man with a face like a gnome, who had in the past been a stable-lad at Newmarket. His name was Jenks, and he was a somewhat morose character who gave the impression that he felt he had come down in the world and really ought to have been doing something better than looking after animals that were so much inferior to those he had formerly worked with. Apparently he had once had dreams of becoming a successful jockey, but nothing had come of it and the disappointment had soured him.

Hector asked Wentworth why he had engaged such a gloomy individual who obviously hated everybody with whom he came into contact.

'Felt sorry for him,' Wentworth said. 'Down on his luck. Out of a job. And wasn't demanding much in the way of wages.'

Hector guessed that it was this last consideration that had counted most in the man's favour. And one thing had to be admitted: Jenks knew his job.

The other employee was a stable-girl; and Wentworth had perhaps engaged her for quite different reasons. She was eighteen years old, blonde, well-built and quite attractive. Hector wondered why someone like her should have chosen to do the rather dirty work of cleaning out stables and grooming horses. Women had of course worked on farms during the war, but they had been doing their bit for King and Country, as others had in munitions factories and so on. But this was different; a sense of duty did not come into it. The fact of the matter was that the girl was simply besotted with horses and asked for nothing better than to spend her days in their company.

Her name was Millie Saunders and she lodged with the Ludkins, who had a spare room now that their only daughter had grown up, married and fled the nest. Millie was the only person Jenks seemed to treat with anything approaching civility. For her he would do anything, and his wrinkled old face would even break into the semblance of a smile when she spoke to him. It was as if the sight of her melted the ice in his heart and caused it to beat faster for a while. Possibly he was even a little bit in love with her. It would not have been surprising.

Jenks slept in the harness-room on a camp bed and ate his meals with the others in the house. The harness-room was in the barn and had a pervading odour of leather and saddle soap and liniment, which Hector found rather pleasant, except when it was polluted with smoke from the cigarettes which Jenks rolled for himself, using a dark stringy tobacco extracted from a tin.

Unlike these employees, who had wages paid to them weekly, Hector received no regular income as a partner in the riding school. When he wanted money he asked Wentworth for an advance and was handed various sums which he assumed went down in the accounts. There was a room in the house which was known as the office. In it was an old roll-top desk, and there were two rickety chairs and a stool and a rusty iron safe. The desk was littered with papers, some spiked, some clipped together, and there were account books and a loose-leaf file, an inkpot, pens and pencils, a blotting-pad and various other pieces of equipment necessary for office work. Everything was in a state of complete disorder, and there were cobwebs and dust everywhere, since Mrs Ludkin was never allowed to go in with her broom and duster in case she should displace something.

Hector seldom went in there either. He detested paperwork and left all this side of the business to Wentworth. He was not sure how much his partner knew about book-keeping and he did not inquire. He never knew exactly what the financial situation was; he imagined the school, once things had started moving, was making a profit, but Wentworth rarely mentioned the subject, though now and then he would remark that things were going pretty well, so Hector concluded that they were on course and that the goldmine was beginning to disgorge its riches even though there was no solid evidence of this.

They had put some small advertisements in the local press, and after a few months had managed to build up a small clientele which they hoped would increase as word got passed round concerning the attractions of the establishment.

'It's the kind of thing that grows naturally once you've planted the seed,' Wentworth said.

He was still full of enthusiasm, and Hector was infected with it. It was really a most pleasant way of making a living. He felt that the thousand pounds had been well invested and he had no regrets. It never occurred to him to reflect that when Harry dished out a few pounds now and then he was simply giving him back some of his own money. That would have been a sordid way of looking at it.

The early clients were exclusively women and children. Men seemed to be singularly uninterested in learning to ride; perhaps because they were too busy earning the money to pay for the lessons their wives and families were taking. The riding was not confined to the meadows at Chestnuts; there were lanes and woodland trails nearby, and the little files of horses and riders became a familiar sight in the neighbourhood.

'We're getting to be known,' Wentworth said. 'We're becoming a feature of the countryside.'

Known or not, as time passed one disturbing fact had to be faced: the number of clients was not steadily increasing as they had hoped it would. It reached a certain figure and then stopped. It seemed that they had got to the limit, and this limit was far short of what they had anticipated. Yet Wentworth refused to be discouraged.

'Early days, old boy, early days. Things'll pick up. Summer's coming in. Holidays and all that.'

Summer indeed came, and the school holidays; but still there was no rush of new pupils. Wentworth put a brave face on things, but Hector noticed that he no longer spoke of buying more horses or extending the stabling. The word now was consolidation, which really meant accepting the situation as it was and forgetting about any expansion for the present at least.

Hector was happy enough. It was a good life, even if he was not getting rich. As for the future, he had never been much bothered with thoughts about that. Live for the day; that was his motto.

Occasionally he went to see his parents, riding into the city on the Douglas motor-cycle. On these occasions his father would always ask about the business in a rather contemptuous manner.

'Made your fortune with those horses yet?'

Hector would have liked to answer: 'Yes; the money is rolling in hand over fist.' It would have taken the wind out of the old man's sails. But it would not have been the truth, and he doubted whether it would have been believed anyway. So he would just give a shrug and change the subject.

His mother never asked any questions about financial matters. She was more concerned with his wellbeing. He assured her he was getting regular meals and was perfectly comfortable at Chestnuts. She had an often repeated complaint that his visits were not frequent enough; but the fact was that he was bored when he was there and only too relieved to get away again. The parental home had a depressing effect on him.

But the depression did not last for a moment after he was out of the house and riding away on the trusty old Douglas. He was really enjoying himself in those late spring and summer days. He liked working with horses; he liked the fresh air, the exercise and the sense of freedom. He even came to like the dilapidated old house and the barn and stables and the view across the meadows to the distant fields and woods. It was a green and pleasant land indeed, in vivid contrast to those muddy shell-pocked fields of France with their gaunt, bare stumps of trees standing up like so many ragged sentinels. These were happy days. How could he not be happy with so much going for him?

And on top of everything else, to cap it all like the fairy at the summit of the Christmas tree, there was Clara.

6

Suggestion

Clara Millbank was the wife of a wealthy Norwich businessman, and she was one of the first clients who came to the riding school. She drove herself there in a gleaming Sunbeam car which had been given to her by her husband as a birthday present. She had no children and plenty of time on her hands to use as she wished while Mr Millbank was busy at his office making more of the cash that subsidised a fairly expensive lifestyle.

Hector could never be quite certain whether he seduced her or she seduced him. Perhaps it had been a little of each, for there could be little doubt that both had been willing to seduce and be seduced. And the opportunity had been there for the taking.

Clara was considerably older than Hector. She never told him what her age was, but he made a guess that it was somewhere around thirty-five. What she did tell him was that her husband was much older than she was and that she had never really been in love with him. Without stating as much in so many

38

words, she managed to give the impression that she had married him for his money and no other reason. What he had received in return was a wife of undoubted charm who could be paraded before the eyes of the world with a deal of pride.

And she was still attractive enough to catch any man's eye. She caught Hector's and he caught hers. Soon she was monopolising his attention to such an extent that Wentworth noticed it.

'That lady's got you in her sights. You'd better watch your step.'

Hector gave a laugh. 'If she has it's all to the good of the business, isn't it?'

'As long as it doesn't go beyond business. Bear in mind she has a husband.'

Hector thought Wentworth was hardly the one to be censorious, for it was certain that he himself was casting more than a passing glance at Millie, and that she was not inclined to give him the brush-off.

'Don't worry,' he said. 'She's too old for me.'

But he knew that this was not true. She was most certainly not too old; it was her maturity that was one of the attractions to a young man of his age. Yet for most of the summer the affair, if such it could have been called, progressed in a rather low-key manner like a sulky fire before suddenly bursting into flame in late August.

They were in a wood, separated from the other riders who were all youngsters on ponies and were accompanied by Millie Saunders. Clara brought her horse to a standstill and Hector followed suit.

She said abruptly: 'Tom's going away for two or three weeks. On business.'

Hector knew that Tom was Mr Millbank, a man whom he had never met and never wished to meet.

'Ah!' he said; and waited, knowing there would be more, knowing that this piece of information had not been thrown out for no particular purpose. It had to be leading up to something.

'I thought — ' she said; and stopped, regarding him with a speculative eye, as if calculating what his reaction might be to words as yet unspoken.

'Yes?' he said. 'What did you think?'

'That you and I might spend a few days in London. It would be fun, don't you think?'

'Yes,' he said, 'I think it might be.'

He felt pretty sure that Harry Wentworth would not object to his going away for a while. After all, it was about time he had a holiday. The snag that immediately sprang to mind, however, was the question of expense.

There were such things as hotel bills, theatre tickets, rail fares, taxis, restaurants and the devil knew what else. A woman like Clara Millbank was hardly likely to be content with a cheap hotel and theatre seats in the gods; she would demand the best. And the best was expensive.

But then she brushed aside any misgivings he might have had with her next words.

'My treat, of course.'

He wondered whether she could really mean what she seemed to be saying: that she would pick up the bill for everything. She seemed to guess what was in his mind and proceeded to remove all his doubts on that score.

'It won't cost you a penny. I've got plenty for both of us.'

'Oh,' he said, 'but I couldn't — '

And even as he said it he knew that he could. And would.

'Now don't be silly,' she said. 'What earthly reason is there why I shouldn't pay? It's so dreadfully old-fashioned to think that the man must always be the provider. You surely aren't going to tell me you would feel dishonoured or something quite ridiculous like that, are you? We're in the twentieth century now. Women are beginning to demand their rights, and about time too.'

He grinned. 'I didn't realize you were such a militant.'

'Oh,' she said, 'there's so much you don't know about me, Hector darling. This could be your opportunity to learn more. But of course if the idea doesn't appeal to you — '

He was quick to reassure her on that point. 'Oh, it appeals to me all right. It appeals to me very much.'

'Well, then?'

She was looking at him with a hint of mockery in her expression, as though she were daring him to accept her offer, and he was sure that if he did not he would be diminished in her estimation. It might even be the end of the affair. And he certainly did not want that; he was too strongly attracted to her. He gazed at her, saw the mockery, saw the loveliness of her, saw the invitation to untold sensual delights and knew that there was no possibility of refusing what he had been offered.

'I think,' he said, 'it would be simply wonderful.'

'And no more stupid objections?'

'No more objections.'

★ ★ ★

He confided in Wentworth. He had not intended to. Indeed, Clara had warned him not to tell anyone about their plan, and he had agreed that secrecy was essential. But Wentworth of course asked why he wanted to get away for a time; and when Hector explained that he was planning to spend a few days in London his partner smelt a rat.

'Going to be on your ownsome?'

'Yes.'

'Not much fun all by yourself.'

'Don't you think so?'

'No, old boy, I don't. You wouldn't be hiding something from me, would you?'

'Such as what?'

'Such as something completely mad. Something like having a rare old time with a certain lady of mature but undoubted charms.'

Hector saw that it would be pointless to try pulling the wool over Wentworth's eyes. When his departure for London coincided with the absence of Clara Millbank from the riding school the connection would be obvious to him. Other people might not notice, but he would.

'All right, Harry; so you've guessed. But keep it under your hat, will you?'

Wentworth gave a disapproving shake of the head. 'You're playing with fire. She's a married woman.'

43

'I know that. And if it comes to the point I'd say you're hardly the one to criticise. At least I'm not cradle-snatching.'

The shot went home. Wentworth reddened and looked angry. 'Now just a minute, Hector. I resent that, I do indeed. I think you should take back that remark.'

Hector immediately regretted what he had said on the spur of the moment; for he had no wish to quarrel with his partner, a man with whom the relationship had generally been a wholly amicable one. It was only recently that Harry Wentworth had appeared to be somewhat touchy, as if there were something on his mind that was bothering him. Anyway, it was not in the best interest of either of them to have a falling-out over a few ill-chosen words.

'All right, I take it back. Shouldn't have said it. Sorry.'

Wentworth was somewhat mollified. 'Apology accepted. When do you propose to leave?'

Hector told him.

'And you'll be away how long?'

'About a week, I imagine.'

'You're not sure?'

'Not really, no.'

It was up to Clara. She was making the arrangements and he was happy to leave all this to her. As she had said, it was her treat.

7

Tooth and Claw

They travelled up to London on different trains to avoid the possibility of being seen together by someone they knew. Hector went on the earlier train and was waiting for her at Liverpool Street Station when she arrived.

'Why, hello there!' she said. 'Fancy meeting you!'

Until that moment he had not felt absolutely certain she would come. She might have had second thoughts, might have realised what a crazy thing she was doing and decided not to go through with it. It would have been an anticlimax, a horrible let-down, but not entirely surprising. And what in hell would he have done then? He had managed to screw thirty pounds out of Harry Wentworth with some difficulty, but what sort of a time could he have had by himself in London on that amount? He would have had to go back and admit to Wentworth that the lady had not turned up. And then another thought had come into his head: had she never intended coming? Perhaps it had all been an elaborate practical joke designed to make a fool of him. Stranger things happened.

So he had remained in a state of suspense during those two hours or so between the arrival of his train and hers and had watched with quickened pulse and no little anxiety the flood of passengers bursting out of the carriages like a human tide. It was not until he saw her and spoke to her that he felt entirely reassured.

'I was afraid you might not come,' he said.

She seemed amazed at the suggestion. 'But darling, why on earth would I not?'

'You might have changed your mind.'

'What absolute nonsense! How could you possibly have imagined such a thing?'

'I don't know. Women do change their minds, so I've heard.'

'And men too. You weren't secretly hoping for that, were you? So that you'd be let off the hook.'

'Now you're the one that's talking non-sense. If there is a hook I like nothing better than being on it.'

'Then stop being such a silly boy,' she said.

It was the first time she had called him a boy, and he did not like it. Certainly in comparison with her he was young, but no one who had been through what he had was any longer a boy, whatever age he might have been. It was a matter of no importance perhaps, but he found it slightly annoying.

★ ★ ★

They took a taxi to the West End hotel where she had booked a room in the name of Mr and Mrs H. Langdon, and that was the beginning of a delightful few days. They went to plays and a Viennese operetta and took a trip on a river boat down to Hampton Court. They visited as many places of interest as could be crammed into so short a space of time: the National Gallery, The Tower, St Paul's, the Zoo, Westminster Abbey and much besides. They strolled in Hyde Park and watched the Changing of the Guard at Buckingham Palace. They ate in the best restaurants and Hector paid for everything with Clara's money. At night they made delirious love and time flew.

But of course it could not last; like all good things it had to come to an end. Though the end, when it did come, was not quite as Hector had foreseen it might be — or indeed as he might have wished it to be.

They had been in London for almost a week when he asked the question: 'When do you propose going back home?'

She had never given any hint as to how long she intended the adventure to continue. He was even ignorant of the length of time for which she had reserved the hotel room; the arrangement had been entirely hers. So it came to him as a complete surprise when she answered quite casually:

'I don't propose going back.'

The full import of what she had said did not immediately get through to him. Perhaps he had misheard.

'I don't understand. What are you saying?'

'I am saying that I have no intention of going back to Norwich. That is plain enough, isn't it?'

'You mean you are going somewhere else first?'

'No,' she said, 'that is not what I mean.'

'But eventually you must go back.'

She smiled. 'Wrong, darling. Quite wrong. There is a note at this moment in Tom's desk, which he will find when he returns. It will tell him that I have left him; that I have gone away with another man; my lover.'

Hector stared at her and felt a sudden chill. He could hardly believe what he had just heard. And yet he had to believe it. And all the possible consequences of her reckless action started to become apparent to him.

'You told him about me?'

'No, darling. I mentioned no name in the letter. He'll just have to guess.'

Hector felt only slightly reassured by this. It would not take Millbank long to discover who his wife's lover was. And then? He dreaded to think what the consequences might be; they were too awful to contemplate.

But there was still time to save the situation. Millbank was not expected to return home for quite a while yet.

'That letter,' he said. 'You've got to get it and burn it before he finds it.'

'But why on earth should I do that? I want him to find it. That's the point, isn't it?'

It began to dawn on him what she had in mind, and it appalled him. It was beyond all reason.

'You don't mean, you can't mean that we — '

'Should make this thing between us permanent? Just you and me? But of course. Why not? We love each other, don't we? So what could be more natural? I don't give a damn what other people may say or think. To hell with them.'

'But it's impossible.'

'I see no reason why it should be. I've got money, you know. I'm not entirely dependent on Tom. Just think what a wonderful life we'll have together. It will be heaven.'

He did think of it, and again he was appalled. It was not what he had ever envisaged for the future. A week or so in London with Clara was one thing; it was fine; but what she was proposing was quite a different matter. Already his ardour had begun to cool somewhat even in these past few days during which they had been together. He had become aware of physical imperfections to which he had previously been blind. That fifteen-year gap between their ages could not be disregarded. And looking into the future, when he was thirty she would be forty-five, possibly more. Moreover, he would be dependent on her for everything; which might be all very well from her point of view, but certainly not from his. He had no desire to be kept by an older woman, or any woman if it came to that. The part of a gigolo was not something he had ever had in mind for himself.

So he said: 'It's not on, you know. It's just not on.'

The coldness of his tone, the expression on his face, not of delight at the prospect but rather of dismay, the entire lack of any enthusiasm with which her vision of lasting mutual bliss had been greeted seemed to strike her like a blow, and her own expression of eager anticipation of his ready acceptance of her proposal gave way to disappointment and even anger.

'Why?'

'Because it's a crazy idea. Sheer unadulterated madness. Can't you see it is?'

'No, I can't.'

'Then you must be a fool.'

He had spoken without thinking and regretted uttering the words almost immediately. But it was too late. Her face darkened, became quite ugly. Her voice was hard and bitter.

'How dare you speak to me like that! How dare you!'

He tried to mend things with an apology. 'I'm sorry. I didn't mean to be so blunt, but it just slipped out.'

'And you think that's enough?'

He shrugged. 'What else can I say?'

'You could say how grateful you are for what I'm offering you. You could say how happy it makes you. You could say there's nothing in the world you want more than to run away with me and live with me for ever.'

'Yes,' he said, 'I could say all that. But of course none of it would be true.'

'I thought you loved me. Damn you, Hector, you told me so, again and again. Was that a lie also? Did you never mean it?'

'At the time, maybe I did.'

'But not now?'

'Look.' he said, 'this is getting us nowhere. It's all so pointless. I can't agree to what you're proposing and there's an end of it. Sorry, Clara, but that's the way it is.'

She seemed to go mad then. She sprang at him like a wildcat, spitting out obscenities such as he had not heard since his army days and would never have expected from her mouth. He was standing by the bed in their room, and her attack on him was so sudden and impetuous that he was caught off balance and thrown backwards on to the mattress. She fell on top of him and he had difficulty in extricating himself. She was beating him furiously with her fists and using her nails to scratch his face. He was sure that if she had had some weapon to hand she would have killed him in her blind rage. He had never seen her in such a frenzy, never imagined she was capable of such an outburst of passion.

He managed to take a grip on her wrists and prevent more of the hitting and scratching. But again she spat at him and even sank her teeth into his bare forearm. Stung by this, he thrust her violently away from him, and she stumbled and fell at the foot of the bed. He stood up and looked down at her, half expecting that she would get up and renew the attack. But she did not; she just lay there, breathing heavily and glowering up at him, all the fight it seemed having gone out of her.

His forearm was bleeding where she had bitten him, and when he touched his left cheek with the tips of his fingers he could feel the wetness of blood there also.

'Well,' he said, 'that was quite an exhibition, but I wouldn't want a replay.'

He was reflecting that it was as well he had refused her invitation to share his life with her. He had told her it was a crazy idea, but he had not realized just how crazy. Now he knew. She could be mad when she did not get her own way, no doubt about that. And he had no wish to live with a mad woman who was liable to attack him whenever he thwarted her desires.

She got up, and he eyed her warily, prepared for a second attack now that she had got her breath back. But the spirit seemed to have gone out of her, and she simply went to a chair and sat down and began to weep.

'No need for that,' he said. 'It's not the end of the world. Life will go on.'

She glared at him through the tears. 'Damn you, Hector. How can you be so calm?'

'I'm not really. I'm seething.' He took out a handkerchief and dabbed his cheek. The cloth came away stained red. 'You certainly put your mark on me. Which is something even the Hun never managed. One up to you.'

A phrase came into his mind: red in tooth and claw. That would seem to describe Clara. She had used both on him. But it would never happen again; he would make sure of that. This was the finish of any relations between them. It was a pity it should have ended like this, on such a low note, but that was the way of things; you could not order them all to your own liking.

'I suppose,' he said, 'we shall not be going to the theatre this evening after all.'

She glared at him again but said nothing.

He left her and went to the bathroom to see what he could do about his savaged face and arm.

8

Unpleasant Incident

'Oh, my God!' Wentworth exclaimed when he saw the scratches on Hector's cheek. 'Whatever happened to you?'

'I was attacked,' Hector said.

'By the lady?'

'If that's what you'd call her.'

'I gather,' Wentworth said, 'you had a falling-out and that's why you're back sooner than planned.'

'Correct.'

'Oh dear! Come into the office and tell me all about it.'

They went into the office and Hector told him all about it. Wentworth listened with ever-increasing amazement.

'You really mean to tell me she proposed that you and she should go away together and live happily ever after?'

'That's about the gist of it.'

'And when you refused she attacked you?'

'Right again.'

'She must have a tile loose.'

'Maddened with love,' Hector said; and he

55

gave a laugh. He could see the funny side of it now, and felt himself lucky to have escaped with nothing worse than a bite and a scratch. 'Must be the effect I have on women. Drives them crazy.'

'I fancy she was crazy from the start. I don't imagine she'll tell old Millbank the story when he comes home.'

'I doubt it. She can't be that crazy.'

'Well, it's bad business from our point of view. I'd say we've lost a good customer. And the way things are going, that's something we can ill afford.'

'Bad as that, is it?'

'I won't mislead you, Hector. The situation could be a damn sight better than it is. We're in a bit of a sticky patch and that's the truth.'

Hector was not altogether surprised to hear this. He had suspected that all was not well at Chestnuts for some time, but Wentworth had never previously admitted as much.

'But we'll pull through?'

'Touch and go, old boy; touch and go.'

Which was not exactly reassuring, Hector thought. Not reassuring at all in fact.

★ ★ ★

It was just four days after his return to work when another unpleasant incident occurred.

56

There had been no sign of Clara Millbank in this time and no communication from her. He assumed that she had returned home, though he had seen nothing of her since their departure from the London hotel. He did not expect ever to see her again; the parting had been so acrimonious that the likelihood of any reconciliation seemed out of the question.

He for his part would certainly make no approach of that kind; he felt that he had had a lucky escape and he had no intention of pushing his luck any further. And as for the lady, it seemed impossible that pride would allow her ever to speak to him again. She had been humiliated by his rejection of her offer, and it would not be easy for her to forget that final scene in the hotel bedroom. Was she ashamed of her behaviour? He neither knew nor cared. It was an episode in his life that was finished, and already he was beginning to look back on it with a certain wry amusement; because really when you came to think about it, it had been rather farcical to say the least.

The second incident involved a man named Charles Saunders, who happened to be the father of Millie Saunders, the stable-girl.

Saunders was a rather stout gentleman

with a face which bore a certain resemblance to a boiled beetroot, both in shape and colour. He was middle-aged and rather quick-tempered, and was one of those men who liked to use the army rank they had attained during the war, even though this had been merely temporary. The rank in Saunders's case was major; and he had a clipped military moustache and a somewhat bulbous eye. He had never in fact been in combat but had been in one of the service units stationed well behind the front line. This was a fact that he seldom felt called upon to mention.

He arrived at Chestnuts one day in a Humber car, and Hector saw him getting out of it. He had never seen the man before, and he thought that this might be a prospective client, though he did not really look like one, apart from the rather odd fact that he was carrying a riding-crop in his right hand. He was wearing a Harris tweed jacket and cavalry twill trousers and a striped tie which might have been that of his old school or maybe some club to which he belonged. He had a broad forehead from which the gingery hair was beating a hasty retreat, and there was an expression on his face which might have denoted determination and not a little anger.

As soon as he got out of his car he spotted Hector and at once headed towards him. He came to a halt a couple of yards or so from the younger man and stared at him with those pop-eyes of his while tapping his right leg with the riding-crop.

'You,' he said. 'What's your name?'

It was hardly the most polite of greetings, and Hector felt inclined to tell him to mind his own business. But perhaps it was his business, so he answered civilly:

'I'm Hector Langdon. What can I do for you?'

'I'm Major Saunders. I believe my daughter works here.'

'Millie. Yes, that's so. You want to see her?'

'Not at the moment. I'm looking for a rat named Harold Wentworth. Can you tell me where he is?'

It was on the tip of Hector's tongue to say that none of the rats about the place had names as far as he knew; but again he curbed his tongue. He was not at all favourably impressed by Saunders, who appeared to be the bullying type; and if he really was Millie's father it was pretty certain that she took after her mother rather than this boor. However, he remained civil, since there was no point in adding fuel to the fire of wrath which already seemed to be burning in the man.

'Mr Wentworth is in the house, I believe.

I'll take you to him if you wish.'

'I certainly do wish,' Saunders said.

'Come this way then.'

They found Wentworth in the office, apparently struggling to deal with a mass of papers scattered over the desk. There was a harassed look about him, and he was certainly not in the happiest of moods when Hector ushered Saunders in. He dropped the pencil he had been using and swivelled round on his chair to face them. Hector thought it best to make the introduction as brief as possible.

'Harry,' he said, 'this is Major Saunders. Millie's father.'

He had never seen Wentworth so disconcerted; it seemed for the moment to throw him completely off balance. But he recovered quickly. He stood up and made a tentative offer of his hand. Saunders pointedly ignored it and the gesture of goodwill came to nothing.

Saunders glared at him, and the eyes seemed to pop even more. 'So,' he said, 'you're the rat.'

'Rat!' Wentworth said. 'What rat would that be?'

'The one that's been playing around with my daughter.'

Hector wondered whether to get out of

there and leave them to it; because he had a feeling that things were turning a trifle nasty and were likely to get worse. But he was interested to observe the outcome of the encounter and he hung on.

It was not difficult to guess at the train of events that had led to the emergence of this Major Saunders, whom neither he nor Harry had ever set eyes on until this moment. Wentworth had not been content with a bit of harmless flirtation with the pretty young stable-girl; he had taken things further, until eventually he had enticed her into his bed. This had probably not been too difficult; it had been easy to see for some time that she was attracted to him; but it had been rather unwise, as he had told Harry. Yet even so there might not have been any serious consequences if the girl had not recently got into the way of spending the night at Chestnuts.

So how did the major come to hear about this? That was an easy one to answer. Millie was lodging with the Ludkins, and Mrs Ludkin could hardly fail to notice that the girl did not always occupy her own bed at night. Acquainted as she was with the situation at Chestnuts, it would not have taken much deduction on her part to make a pretty shrewd guess as to what was happening. For a time perhaps she had overlooked the matter, not wishing to jeopardise her own employment; but the Ludkins were devout chapelgoers, and no doubt eventually the contest between conscience and self-interest had ended in favour of the former and she had decided to inform Major Saunders of what was going on.

The result was this visit from that irate gentleman.

'Now look,' Wentworth said. 'Let's not start being rude to each other. I resent being called a rat.'

'I could think of worse things to call you,' Saunders told him. 'Do you deny that you have corrupted my daughter?'

Wentworth had quite regained his self-possession now that the initial shock of the major's appearance on the scene had worn off. So he said:

'Corrupted her? No, I wouldn't say that. Corruption's a pretty strong word, don't you think?'

'To my mind it's not a bit too strong. Do you or do you not admit that you have seduced her?'

'Now there again,' Wentworth said, 'it depends on what you mean by seduction. If two people like each other well enough to go to bed together by mutual consent, who is the seducer? Both or neither? It's a moot point, I'd say.'

When he had finished this little speech he gave a smirk, and it was probably this as much as the words that really incensed the already angry Saunders.

'Damn you!' he said.

And he struck Wentworth on the left cheek with the riding-crop.

It would, Hector reflected, have been more appropriate if it had been a horsewhip. A thorough horsewhipping was the classic form of retribution meted out by an angry father to the corrupter of his daughter. Possibly Saunders would have used the whip if he had had one available; but in the absence of such a weapon he had been forced to make do with the inferior implement.

Not that it was so much less effective. Judging by Wentworth's reaction, the blow must have stung. He gave a cry in which anger and pain seemed to be equally mixed, and before Saunders could repeat the blow he lashed out at him with his fist.

It was the major's chin that took the impact, and it staggered him. But he recovered quickly and tried to use the riding-crop again. Wentworth blocked this move by grabbing his wrist, and the two men struggled with each other, grunting with the effort and blundering around in the rather limited space.

Hector, feeling that things had gone quite far enough, decided to intervene. He wrenched the riding-crop from Saunders's grasp and called on the contestants to stop.

'Cut it out! You're behaving like a couple of kids. Don't be so damned stupid.'

Rather to his surprise, they heeded his admonition. They were possibly not at all sorry to bring to an end a struggle in which neither seemed to be gaining any advantage. They broke away from each other, breathing hard and scowling.

'That's better,' Hector said. 'Now why not talk things over like sensible adults?'

In fact there was little to talk over. Saunders said he was going to take his daughter away from Chestnuts and Wentworth just shrugged, as much as to say that he was not bothered. There was a red weal on his cheek where the crop had struck him, and he fingered it tenderly. Much of Saunders's ire seemed to have evaporated; possibly he felt that though he had inflicted only one lash with the crop it could be taken to be symbolical of a horsewhipping and honour was thereby satisfied.

Millie, who had been working with Jenks in the barn, was unaware that her father was on the premises until Hector went to fetch her. When it dawned on her that she was being taken away from the riding school, and perhaps more especially from Harry Wentworth, she was not at all pleased. In fact she refused point-blank to leave. It was not until Wentworth told her bluntly she had to go that she came to the bitter realization that she had no alternative and must accept the situation as it was.

She departed in her father's car, weeping floods of tears and obviously not in the least consoled by Wentworth's parting suggestion that it was all for the best and she would soon get over it.

When the car had gone Hector said: 'You're going to miss her, I imagine.'

Wentworth grinned. 'About as much as you're missing Clara Millbank. Fact is, old boy, she was becoming a bit of a pain in the neck. Had this odd idea that I was going to marry her. Not on the cards. Not on the cards at all.'

'I see. Well, I know one person who will miss her.'

'Who's that?'

'Jenks.'

'Ah yes. He does seem to have been rather gone on her.'

'If you ask me,' Hector said, 'the old fellow is in love with her.'

'Now that,' Wentworth said, 'really would be crazy.'

9

A Target Again

It seemed to Hector that everything was happening, if not entirely at once, at least in the course of a very few days. First there had been that unforgettable business in London which had resulted in the loss of a valuable client. This had been closely followed after his return by the confrontation with Major Saunders and the tearful departure of the charming stable-girl. And as if these two disasters were not enough to be going on with, three days later Wentworth informed him that the riding school would have to be closed down.

This information might have come as more of a shock to Hector if he had not had that earlier hint from his partner that all was by no means well with the enterprise. When Wentworth had told him that it was touch and go whether they would pull through he had been understating the seriousness of the situation. He must have known even then that the school had reached the end of its tether.

'So it's really come to that, has it?'

'Afraid so. Sorry, old boy. Should never have dragged you into this mess. But I had hopes. I did have great hopes that we'd make a go of it.'

'And there's no chance of carrying on?'

'None whatever. The vultures are gathering. Shylock is demanding his pound of flesh. Not that there's much flesh left for him to take.'

Wentworth gradually revealed the full extent of the disaster. The salient point was that he was bankrupt. The property was mortgaged, he was up to the ears in debt and was overdrawn at the bank. Hector's thousand pounds had of course gone down the drain.

He had the grace to look sheepish when he admitted this.

'Wretched business. Thought it might just prime the pump and all that. Wasn't enough of course. Might have been if we'd had more clients. Maybe we were before our time. The thing simply didn't catch on in a big way. Pity, but there it is. I've let you down, Hector; that's what bothers me most. I don't give a damn about the creditors; they can go to hell for all I care. But I truly am sorry about that money of yours. What a swine it all is.'

'Don't let it worry you,' Hector said. 'Some you win and some you lose. That's life. And besides, I had some of it back, didn't I?'

'That's true.'

'And there was the experience. Can't put a price on that, can you?'

Wentworth grinned. 'That's true as well. Even if it did result in a scratched cheek. You can never say the lady failed to leave her mark on you.'

'Or Millie's angry pa on you.'

'That too,' Wentworth said; and he laughed. 'What a pair we've been, you and I, Hector. I'm going to miss you. What will you do?'

'That's a good question,' Hector said. 'And I don't yet know the answer. One thing's certain: there's a lot of living still to come.'

'You hope.'

'Yes, I hope. But who can tell?'

He asked Wentworth whether Jenks had been told that there was no longer a job for him at Chestnuts.

'Not yet,' Wentworth said.

'It'll be a shock to him.'

'He'll survive. He's a tough nut.'

'But where will he find another job? A man of his age.'

'That's his problem. I've got enough of my own without bothering my head about his.'

Which was a bit hard on Jenks, Hector thought. He felt sorry for the man. Not much in the future for him. No doubt he imagined he had found a snug little billet, and now this.

He accompanied Wentworth when he decided to go and break the news to Jenks. The man was nowhere about the yard. They looked in the stables and he was not there.

'Maybe he's in the barn,' Hector suggested. 'Could be.'

They went into the barn and Wentworth gave a shout, but there was no answer.

'How about the harnessroom,' Hector said. 'It's his snuggery after all.'

They went to the harnessroom and Jenks was there sure enough. And it was evident at once why he had not answered the call. No one with a noose round his neck and his feet six inches from the floor was going to hear you however loudly you shouted. And even if he had heard he could not have made any reply. The rope was tied to a beam and there was an overturned iron pail not far from the dangling feet.

'Oh, my God!' Hector exclaimed.

It was not by a long chalk the first dead man he had seen, but it shocked him nevertheless.

Wentworth seemed less affected by the gruesome sight. 'Well now,' he said, 'I've often heard of people kicking the bucket, but this is the first time I've come across anyone who really did it.'

There could be no doubt that it was what Jenks had done. He must have stood on the upended pail in order to slip the noose over his head, and then he had kicked it away so that he hung by the neck and slowly strangled. It was a painful way to die, and it was of no use having second thoughts once the support had gone; there could be no calling it back.

'I wonder why.'

'Well, he hadn't much to live for, had he? No job, no hope, nothing to look forward to except old age and destitution.'

'But,' Wentworth said, 'he didn't know he was out of a job. I hadn't told him.'

'Maybe he could read the signs. And then there was that other thing.'

'What other thing?'

'Millie.'

'Oh, come now. You can't really think he killed himself because she'd gone.'

'Stranger things have happened. Maybe she was the one bright spot left in his life, and when she left it really got to him. The light just went out.'

'Well we'll never know now, one way or the other. Because it's sure as fate he'll not be telling.'

★ ★ ★

Arthur Langdon was not at all surprised to learn that the Chestnuts Riding School had come to the end of its brief life and that Harry Wentworth was bankrupt. Nor was he in the least reticent about saying: 'I told you so.'

'You should have listened to me. I did warn you; but of course you knew better. Well, I hope you've learned your lesson now. I'm only sorry you've thrown away a thousand pounds of your mother's money in the process.'

'Well, at least there's one consolation,' Hector said. 'If I'd taken your advice there'd have been a formal contract of partnership and I'd now have been bankrupt too.'

His father made no comment on this.

And it was only a small consolation, and he regretted the loss. He saw now that he had been far too easily taken in by Wentworth's seductive words regarding the prospects of the riding school. Had Wentworth himself honestly believed in the success of which he spoke so enthusiastically? Possibly. But he had concealed the fact that the property was mortgaged up to the hilt and that he himself was already in debt. Hector's thousand pounds had given things a boost and some

72

money had flowed in from the pupils. But it had never been enough, as he might have seen for himself if he had taken the trouble to examine the accounts — such as they were.

Well, it had been pretty good while it lasted. He had enjoyed it, even if it had ended on a sour note. His one regret was the loss of his mother's money. He had a stab or two of conscience over that, though he had genuinely imagined at the time that it was not at risk. At least, not much.

Not that Frances Langdon appeared to be in the least upset by the loss, though of course she was sorry for Hector's sake that his great hopes had come to nothing. She was shocked to hear about the suicide of Jenks and supposed that it must have been worry over the loss of his job that had driven him to it. Hector thought it advisable not to mention Millie Saunders and the visit of the enraged parent. Similarly, he kept his ill-omened affair with Clara Millbank a secret. That too might have shocked his mother and brought more censure from his father.

'Well,' Arthur Langdon said, 'what do you intend to do now? Have you any more plans for getting rich quick?'

'Not for the moment. I'll scout around. Something is bound to turn up.'

★ ★ ★

Surprisingly, what turned up was recruitment in a body of men commonly known as the Black-and-Tans. This was an armed auxiliary police force stationed in Ireland for the purpose of helping to keep an uneasy peace and put a check on the operations of the IRA. The name came from the khaki uniform and the black cap and armlet.

Hector thought it sounded exciting and volunteered for service. With his army record behind him he found no difficulty in being accepted.

Neither of his parents approved of the move. His father thought it was demeaning for a son of his to become a common policeman; and though Hector argued that this was quite different from being a bobby on the beat in England, Arthur Langdon was not impressed. Hector was still proving to be a great disappointment to him.

His mother regretted the move for quite a different reason. She was concerned for his safety. Ireland had always been such a troublesome part of the British Isles, had it not? Scarcely civilised in fact. Had he not been shot at enough by the Germans that now he had to go making himself a target again?

Neither objection had any effect on Hector, who as he grew older seemed to become more and more headstrong, more and more determined to go his own way without consideration for anyone else. And as to the danger, he dismissed that out of hand. If the unspeakable Hun had been unable to kill him, what did he have to fear from a parcel of crazy Irishmen?

It was perhaps a rash remark to make. Some people might have said it was tempting fate. But he himself would have regarded that as mere superstition. What possible effect could any words uttered by him have on the future?

'Well,' his mother said as she bade him farewell, not without some shedding of tears, 'be careful, Hector dear. Do be very careful.'

He promised that he would. Promises were easy to make.

10

A Close One

They were a pretty rough crowd, those armed auxiliary policemen with whom he found himself in Dublin. They were not squeamish regarding the methods they used in combating civil disorder, and they were detested by the Irish Catholics just as Cromwell's brutal soldiery had been detested in days long gone by.

Hector had been prepared for some brutality, but there were methods used by the Black-and-Tans that revolted even him. The torture of prisoners for instance, which certainly took place, though he never had any hand in it. And there was the burning of cottages by gangs of the B-and-Ts who roamed the countryside armed with service rifles, and the murder of innocent people as reprisals for IRA atrocities. Some of it really stuck in his craw, and there were times when he regretted his impetuosity in joining such a rabble. But he was in it now and had to go through with it.

And the fact was of course that the

methods used to stifle resistance attracted an equally brutal reaction form the IRA. There was butchery on both sides, and it was no rare event to find the body of a Black-and-Tan floating in the Liffey.

They lived in barracks like an army unit, and no one went on patrol alone. Hector found himself paired with a man named Leonard Butcher, a black-haired hulking man of no great intelligence. He had also served in the infantry in the Great War and a bullet had gone through his right cheek, leaving him with a permanent scar and a curiously lopsided appearance. It had damaged his palate too, so that he spoke in a snuffling kind of way that sometimes made it difficult to understand what he was saying, especially when he was excited.

Butcher thought the Irish job was a doddle after the trenches. He had been out of work for some time and was glad enough to pick up any kind of employment. He was particularly disenchanted with the politicians, who had in his opinion done very little to reward the ex-service men after all they had gone through for their country. Lloyd George especially came in for criticism.

'Promised a land fit for heroes to live in, di'n't he? So where is it, I'd like to know? They're all the same, them lot. Promise you the earth when they want anything from you, but forget about you when you're no more use to 'em. Sods!'

In company with Butcher, Hector patrolled the streets of Dublin and kept his eyes skinned for any suspicious movement which might betray the presence of a lurking gunman. There were snipers around, and you never knew when you might get a bullet in the back. It was all so different from that other business which had employed his services on the Continent. Butcher might call it a doddle, but really it was far from that. There might not be the mud and the vermin, minniewerfers and hand grenades and creeping barrages, but death stalked the lanes and alleys and gazed down from upstairs windows.

Yet on the whole Hector enjoyed it. It was one more adventure to take in his stride, and he was adventurous by nature. He did not expect this particular employment to last long, but that did not bother him. He took things as they came and lived for the moment.

★ ★ ★

A reminder of the constant danger in which he was living came one day when he and

Butcher came under fire from some gunmen ensconced in a churchyard. There was a low wall surrounding the place, and the men were using it for cover. Daylight was fading at the time, and it might have been this and the fact that the men had handguns only that saved them, for there were plenty of bullets flying around.

Hector and Butcher were on the opposite side of the road from the wall when the gunmen popped up and started shooting, and it was not the time to start swapping bullets with men who were protected by a brick wall and probably had the advantage in numbers.

'Let's get to hell out of it,' Hector said.

He started running immediately. Butcher stayed a moment to loose off a couple of shots with his revolver at the heads just visible above the wall, then turned and ran too. There had been a few people around when the shooting started, but they had all vanished like ghosts at cock-crow, and now there was no one to be seen.

There were houses on the left, and a narrow lane branched off in that direction. As soon as he came to it Hector took the turning, since it offered shelter from the bullets that were still coming from the churchyard. Butcher followed and had just reached the corner when he gave a cry and dropped his revolver. Hector came to a stop and turned, fearing that his partner might have been seriously wounded. But Butcher was still on his feet and swearing like the devil, so it seemed that no great harm had come to him. He stopped swearing and shouted at Hector to get moving again.

'The sods are coming over the wall.'

He left the revolver where it had fallen and lumbered along behind Hector who was pressing ahead at a pretty good rate. There were houses on each side, light showing in many of the windows but all the doors shut; and then, fifty yards further on, the lane came to a dead end.

Butcher started cursing again, and with some reason. It was hardly the best of situations. Glancing back they could see that the gunmen were coming round the corner of the lane and at any moment they might start up again with the shooting. Moreover, there was now only Hector's revolver to oppose them. As if to add to the misery it had started to rain, and the light had faded even more. There was just one streetlamp in the lane, and it was not working.

Hector thought of beating on the door of one of the houses and demanding shelter, but he doubted whether anyone would have let them in. They might have kicked open the door, but there was no time.

Then Butcher spoke urgently: 'This way! Quick!'

He had spotted a footpath running between the last house on the left and the one blocking the end of the cul-de-sac. They had no idea where it might lead, but the shooting had started again and anything was better than staying where they were. Butcher was already heading down the path, and Hector followed.

The footpath was narrow, winding and muddy, with puddles here and there. The rain was coming on harder, and it had become so dark that it was difficult to see more than a few yards ahead; but this handicap applied equally to the pursuers, who were no longer using their guns but were apparently concentrating their efforts on the task of overtaking the two policemen. There was no doubt in Hector's mind that if they succeeded in doing so they would show no mercy; they were not in the business of taking prisoners but of killing.

Butcher was still ahead of him, but his pace had slackened and he was breathing heavily. Hector could easily have gone ahead of him and left him behind. It would have been a way of saving his own skin, for he could have got clean away while the gunmen were dealing with his partner. But it was an option he did not contemplate for a moment. He had no great liking for Butcher, but that made no difference; he was a comrade and could not be abandoned.

The footpath appeared to have come to a piece of wasteland, and it took a bend to the right and then sloped steeply upward for several yards before descending again. It was apparent that they had crossed a low ridge, and glancing back Hector realized that for the moment they were completely hidden from the pursuers.

He grabbed Butcher's arm and brought him to a halt. Butcher started to protest, but Hector ignored this.

'Follow me,' he said. 'Leave the path.'

He began to run along the base of the ridge and just hoped that Butcher would have the sense to follow. They needed to get well away from the footpath before the gunmen came to the top of the ridge. Then with luck they would not be noticed in the murk, and the others would plough straight on.

The move seemed to work. Butcher made no more protest but fell in behind. A few seconds later the sound of voices could be heard, but turning his head Hector could get no sight of the men; the drenching rain and the gathering darkness had cut visibility almost to nothing.

He ran on, with Butcher lumbering along behind, and the sound of voices faded. He had no idea where he was going, but would just have to trust to luck. And for the moment the luck held. It held until he suddenly felt the ground giving way beneath him and realized that he had blundered into a bog or something of that description. Before he could draw back or utter a warning Butcher had ploughed into it also.

'Bloody hell!' Butcher cried. 'What's this?'

Hector felt no inclination to answer the question; Butcher's guess was as good as his. Whatever it was, he had no doubt that it was imperative to get out of it as quickly as possible. He managed to turn, but he had sunk in up to his knees, and when he tried to move back to more solid ground he fell forward on to his face in the mud. It nauseated him with the stench, and he was floundering for a while; but finally he was able to drag himself out of the mire by grasping some tufts of coarse grass with his outstretched hands.

He lay there on his stomach, gasping for breath and spitting out some of the filth that had got into his mouth. But soon he became aware that Butcher was still in trouble and calling for help.

'All right, all right,' he said. 'Keep your voice down. Do you want that other lot to hear you?'

Butcher lowered his voice but still sounded panicky. 'I'm stuck. I can't get out.'

'Well, give me your hand.'

He could faintly discern the hand that Butcher stretched out, and guessed that it was not the one that the bullet had hit; if in fact he had been hit in the hand and not the arm. He lay on his stomach and could just reach it. He pulled, but could not maintain his grip, and the two slimy hands slipped apart.

'Oh, Gawd!' Butcher mumbled. 'I'm a goner.'

'Don't talk daft,' Hector said. 'Hook your fingers; that's the way. So they don't slip.'

He reached out again with his own fingers and locked them into Butcher's. This time the grip held, and slowly he managed to draw the man towards him. The bog tried to hold its victim but was unable to do so. After a minute or two of desperate struggle Butcher emerged from the mire with a glutinous sucking sound and lay panting on the ground at Hector's side.

'Thanks, mate,' he said when he had got his breath back. 'That was a bloody near thing. I ain't been in mud like that since the

Somme. What do we do now?'

'Now,' Hector said, 'we go home.'

But which way was it? That was the question. To go back to the path they had left would be to risk encountering the gunmen once again, but to head in any other direction could well lead to another mire or becoming completely lost. After some deliberation they decided that it would have to be the footpath.

'Let's go,' Hector said.

Butcher gave a sigh and got to his feet, grumbling about the pain in his hand where he had been shot. It was still raining heavily, and a cold wind was blowing. They plodded back the way they had come, keeping the shadowy ridge on the right. The difficulty now was to find the path. It had not been particularly well marked, and now in the rain and the darkness they might well pass completely over it without being aware of the fact.

After a while Butcher said: 'I think we've gone past it.'

Hector was inclined to agree. They seemed to have walked farther than the distance they had covered when going in the opposite direction. They had been running then, but they had not gone very far before stumbling into the bog. So had they now come too far, missing the path altogether?

They came to a halt, uncertain whether to go forward or retreat. And as they were hesitating they heard the sound of voices.

'It's them coming back,' Butcher said. 'Now what?'

The instinct was to run away; but they had tried that once and the result had not been a happy one. This time it might be better to try a different plan. At least Hector thought so. He spoke softly.

'Let's lie down. With luck they won't spot us.'

He thought Butcher might argue, but he did not. In a moment they were both lying on their stomachs, faces to the ground. The voices were coming nearer.

It was a gamble. Hector knew it, and of course Butcher knew it too. They had no idea how far they were from the footpath; there was even a possibility that they were lying right across it and that the returning gunmen would stumble over them. The voices sounded much louder now, and Hector could detect the anger in them. The men were being soaked by the same rain that was soaking him and Butcher, and they were not enjoying it either. Somehow the fugitives had eluded them, and they did not like it; perhaps they were blaming one another for the fiasco.

They were not running; there would have

been no point in it for them now. But still the sound of their approach grew louder, and Hector began to think that the worst might indeed be about to happen. Even if the men did not step on him and Butcher they might pass so close by that they could not help noticing the two dark shapes lying like logs at the side of the track.

A few moments later the men were so close that it was possible to catch some of their words, and it was evident that there was a lot of fairly heated bickering going on. And then it must have developed into more than mere words; the entire party had come to a stop, and there seemed to be a deal of jostling going on and possibly blows being struck. Hector was keeping his face to the ground and could see nothing; but he could tell that the party had halted within a few feet of where he was lying. He could only hope that, being so engrossed in their own dispute, they would not glance down and see what was there at their feet.

He heard a squelching sound, and something touched him lightly on the left shoulder. He guessed that it was a man's foot, possibly the heel, and he was sure that the game was up. And with the gunmen in their present angry mood it was a virtual certainty that they would not hesitate to carry out a summary execution.

He waited for the shout that would announce discovery and the bullets that would follow swiftly after. But miraculously nothing of the kind occurred. He could still hear the squelching of feet in the mud and the hard breathing of the struggling men; and still he waited for the fatal discovery to be made; knowing that it was inevitable.

But then one of the men said: 'Ah, cut it out, boys, cut it out. Why be fightin' ourselves, for God's sake? Let's be gettin' on home before the bloody rain drowns the lot of us.'

The words seemed to have their effect. The sounds of struggling and bickering ceased; and a moment later the whole party set off again. Very soon there was no more to be heard of them.

Hector and Butcher got to their feet.

'That was a close one,' Butcher said. 'I thought they'd have seen us for sure.'

'One of them touched me with his foot.'

'The devil he did! And never noticed. Somebody up there must be watching over us.'

'I wouldn't bet on it,' Hector said. 'I surely wouldn't bet on it.'

11

Fated

Whenever he was off duty and went out on the town Hector discarded his uniform and wore plain clothes. He hoped that in this guise no one would recognise him as a member of the hated Black-and-Tans.

On these outings he steered clear of those public houses which were known to be the haunts of hardline republicans. He also tried to avoid the company of Lennie Butcher; he saw enough of the man when on duty. But sometimes Butcher could be difficult to shake off. He seemed unable to grasp the fact that anyone could not help being delighted to have him around.

Neither of them were in very good odour with their superiors after the encounter which had so nearly cost them their lives. There was no sympathy whatever for them, and plenty of blame.

A certain Inspector McClair was particularly scathing when they were interviewed by him. By this time they had washed the mud off themselves and were in clean uniforms.

Butcher had also had his wound, such as it was, treated and bandaged.

McClair's first words were hardly encouraging. He fixed them with a bloodshot eye and said:

'Well, you're a fine bloody pair, and no mistake.'

The inspector was a tough, hard-bitten character with a nice line in invective. He was not loved by any of his subordinates, who generally referred to him as 'that old bastard'. His attitude to most of them was one of ill-concealed contempt.

For Hector Langdon and Leonard Butcher at this moment there was no attempt whatever to hide the contempt. All efforts at excusing themselves were brushed aside. The fact that they had been ambushed by a party of gunmen with the advantage of numbers and had only narrowly escaped with their lives cut no ice with him. His reading of the incident was that it was their ineptitude that had led them to walk into the trap, and their pusillanimity that had induced them to run away from the Irishmen.

'Is that what you think you're here for? Is that what your country pays you to do?'

The most heinous crime of all was Butcher's losing of his revolver.

'So you make a gift of one more weapon to

the bloody IRA. Very generous of you. No doubt you'll get a vote of thanks. But not from me, you useless article.'

It was of no use Butcher's pointing out that he had been shot in the hand and forced to drop the revolver. The fact that his wound was little more than a scratch weakened his case. It was not even bad enough to get him excused duty.

'One day I'm going to knock that bugger's teeth in,' Butcher confided to Hector after they had been dismissed from the inspector's presence with fleas in their ears. 'One day he'll get my fist right in his gob.'

'And where will that get you?' Hector said. 'In the slammer. Wouldn't be worth it.'

'Maybe it would at that,' Butcher said.

But Hector felt sure he would never do it. Inspector McClair was just one of those unpleasantnesses you had to live with.

★   ★   ★

He met Noreen O'Hare one day when he was unencumbered by the presence of Leonard Butcher. It was a fine evening, and he would always remember that meeting, not only for the way it had come about, but also for the consequences that were to stem from it. For the consequences were dire indeed, though

91

he had no inkling of this at the time.

It was really odd, that encounter; unexpected, unforeseen; fated perhaps. Certainly fateful. And the manner of it was a simple collision between two people. He bumped into her on the pavement of O'Connell Street — literally. It almost threw her off her feet. To save her from falling he reached out a hand and grabbed her arm.

'Oh,' he said, 'I'm so sorry. I didn't look where I was going.'

'Nor I,' she said. 'It happens.'

She was wearing a hat, but he scarcely noticed it; he was too enchanted by the face beneath it. This was so lovely he wanted to take it in his hands and draw it to him and kiss the lips. But he knew that would have been fatal. She would have run from him.

Or would she?

Their eyes met, and something must have passed between them like a current of electricity, invisible but no less perceptible for that. He felt it, and she was to tell him later that she felt it too. For perhaps a quarter of a minute neither of them spoke; they stood there motionless, as if frozen, gazing raptly at each other. In the end it was she who broke the spell.

'Well, I must be going now.'

'No,' he said. 'Don't go!'

'And why would I not?' she asked.

'Because — ' he said; and stopped, not knowing what reason to give, except the one that was the truth. And then saying that anyway. 'Because I don't want you to.'

She laughed at that. And it was such a low, sweet laugh, seeming to match the soft Irish brogue of her voice, that he was enchanted the more. So he laughed too, and said:

'Well, it was the only reason I could think of.'

'But I can't just stand here forever. That would not be sensible at all.'

'Then may I come with you?'

'Not knowing where it would lead you?'

'Not knowing and not caring.'

'Are you mad?' she said.

'Probably.'

'Well, maybe I'm a little that way inclined myself,' she said. 'So what's your name, madman?'

'Hector Langdon. And I'm English.'

'I won't hold it against you, for it's not your fault; it's the way you were born. And I'm Noreen O'Hare. Irish.'

'As if I hadn't guessed.'

'Shall we go then?'

She began to walk and he fell in beside her.

★ ★ ★

That was how it started. After that they spent as much time together as they could. He had to explain his continued presence in Dublin; he could not say he was just there on a visit. So he told her he was gathering material for a novel he was planning to write. It was to have an Irish setting and he was there doing research. She accepted the story without question, and he felt rather guilty about lying to her. But to have told her the true reason for his presence there would have been to kill their relationship stone dead.

Butcher guessed that something was going on. Hector would never agree now to accompany him when off duty.

'I do believe you've found yourself an Irish tart,' he said.

'You're wrong,' Hector said. 'I have not found an Irish tart. And what I do in my spare time is none of your damned business.'

'All right, all right,' Butcher said, obviously taken aback by this unexpectedly sharp reaction to his suggestion. 'Keep your hair on. Good luck to you, whatever it is, I say. But mind your step. This isn't London, you know.'

★ ★ ★

94

Now that Noreen had walked into his life police duties seemed just a chore that had to be got through as the price to be paid for his time with her. She had told him very little about herself. She said she worked in an office, but she did not not say what kind of office it was and he did not ask; it was not important. They had their agreed meeting-place but had not other means of getting in touch with each other. It was as though the haziness of their backgrounds added to the attraction that had drawn them together. For each of them there was this mystery surrounding the other, and it was as though both hesitated to bring about any change for fear it might shatter the dream world in which they were living.

She became his guide to the city, and he enjoyed it more for the company of the person who was conducting him than for anything that might figure in the itinerary; though there was indeed much to admire.

One day he said: 'It's true what the old song says.'

'And what would that be?' she asked.

'In Dublin's fair city, where the girls are so pretty. Isn't that the way it goes?'

'Ah,' she said, 'but I'm no fishmonger, I'll have you know.'

'Perhaps that's as well. I doubt whether the

sweetness of Miss Malone had anything to do with the odour of her. Not after handling all those fish. She couldn't have had a very pleasing scent.'

'And I have?'

'Everything about you is pleasing to me,' he said. 'I dream about you every night.'

She gave him a quizzing glance. 'Is that the truth now, or is it just the blarney you're giving me?'

'Oh, it's not blarney. I'm English, you know, not Irish.'

'That's true, But maybe there's English boys can use the blarney when it suits them.'

'Not this one. Not in this case. You must know I'm crazy about you.'

'Yes,' she said, 'maybe I do know. And I think maybe we're both a bit crazy.' She was serious now, and all the laughter had gone. 'For where is it all leading? That's what I ask myself. What does the future hold for us? Will you tell me that?'

It was a question he had asked himself many times. And he had no answer to it. This fair city of Dublin was a troubled one, and its future was as uncertain as theirs. The political situation had never interested him much, even though it touched him closely. Eamon De Valera and Michael Collins and the rest of the Sinn Fein leaders were mere names to him, and the fact was that he personally did not give a damn whether Ireland became an independent state or not.

It was a subject that he and Noreen never discussed. He had no idea what her views were on that matter and whether or not she felt at all strongly about it. She had given no hint that she did, and he had studiously avoided ever steering their conversation in that direction. He suspected it might prove to be a minefield that could blow up in his face.

Then suddenly she said: 'I think it's time you met my family.'

And this was something else that had never been mentioned; something too that he had feared might eventually come up. He had not wanted it to; he had no wish to meet her family; he would have liked things to go on just as they were. But he knew that this was not on the cards. The time had been certain to come when she would feel that a move must be made to clarify the situation.

'Ah!' he said. 'So it's come to that.'

She could not fail to notice his lack of enthusiasm.

'Do you not want to?'

'I think it could be something of an ordeal.'

'Why so? They're nice people.'

'They may not approve of me, though. Have you thought of that?'

'Oh, I'm sure they will.'

'Have you told them about me?'

'Not yet.'

'Why not?'

'Oh, I don't know. It just didn't seem necessary.'

He guessed that the reason was more than this. She probably had her own doubts about the family's reaction to her involvement with an Englishman who was a complete stranger to them all. She might express confidence that they would accept him without question, but he felt sure that she too was far from certain about this.

'So why is it necessary now?'

'Well, it must come to it sometime, mustn't it? That's if you're really serious about us. About where we go from here, I mean. Are you, Hector?'

'Yes,' he said. 'Yes, I am.'

And even as he said it he wondered whether it was the truth. Because he had never looked beyond the moment, never even considered the possibility of anything permanent like marriage; which was obviously what was in her mind. So now when he did think of it he could see so many obstacles in the way of anything of the sort that it seemed to be an utter impossibility. Yet now that this suggestion of meeting the O'Hares had come up he saw that if he refused to go along with it Noreen must surely take the refusal as an indication that, despite his protestations, he was indeed not serious about where their relationship was heading. And she might break it off there and then, in disillusion.

So it seemed to have come to a choice: either agree to meet the family or see no more of her. She had not said as much, but he had a feeling that it was implied. And he did not want to lose her. It was she who had made this period of auxiliary police duty in Ireland more than simply endurable. Without her what would he have to look forward to? Pub crawls with Lennie Butcher? It did not bear thinking about.

She was watching him rather anxiously, he thought.

Then she said: 'So you will come? You will meet them?'

'Yes,' he said, 'I'll meet them.'

12

Family Gathering

It was a fairly large house, possibly Victorian, rather dilapidated. There was a sizeable garden surrounding it, but this was unkempt and neglected, a veritable wilderness. The place might once have been quite a fashionable residence, but appeared to have come down in the world.

On their way there Noreen had told Hector that her father had been a customs officer, but had had an accident at work which had necessitated the amputation of his left leg, and he had been forced to take early retirement on a reduced pension. She had three brothers: Sean, Niall and Patrick. Sean was the eldest; he was married and living in a different part of Dublin. Niall and Patrick were working, but still living at the family home.

Only Mr and Mrs O'Hare were at home when Hector and Noreen arrived. Rory O'Hare was a smallish man with a thick mat of white hair and a face that might once have been chubby but had rather fallen in on itself.

He had an artificial leg and walked with a stick. His wife Maeve was a faded sort of woman; there was nothing really noteworthy about her. She seemed to live in the shadow of the man, and maybe she felt that she had done her duty in life by bearing and bringing up four children; a task which had perhaps drained much of the spirit out of her.

The introduction took place in a cold, tiled entrance hall; and then they all went into the drawing-room, in which the furniture seemed to have aged with the house. There was a well-worn carpet on the floor and heavy curtains of a dark green colour at the windows. These, with the drearily-patterned wallpaper and smoke-grimed ceiling, combined to lend a gloomy aspect to the room, which Hector found singularly depressing. His spirits had not been high before entering the house, and once he was inside they took a further dip.

They all sat down, Mr and Mrs O'Hare in armchairs and Hector and Noreen side by side on a sofa in which the springs made a faintly musical sound when they moved. As he sat there he could sense an air of suspicion if not plain hostility in the one-time customs officer. He had come prepared for an interrogation, and this was what he got. He supposed it was only natural that the O'Hares would want to know all about him.

'So you're English,' O'Hare said; making it sound like an accusation of some misdemeanour.

'Guilty,' Hector said. And he gave a laugh which no one echoed or even smiled at. Nationality was evidently not considered a joking matter.

'From London, would it be?'

'No. I come from Norwich.' And then, in case their knowledge of the geography of England was not too good: 'That's in Norfolk.'

'I know where Norwich is,' O'Hare said acidly. 'Don't be getting the idea that because we're Irish we're all as ignorant as pigs.'

'I'm sure you're not,' Hector said. And he was thinking: Not ignorant but touchy. Better mind my step.

'I'm told you're writing a book. Is that so, now?'

'Not actually writing it yet. Gathering material.'

'Why here?'

'It seemed as good a place as any.'

It was a pretty feeble reason, and he could tell that O'Hare was not very impressed with it. But he said nothing.

Mrs O'Hare said: 'It's a terrible place just now; a terrible place, sure it is.' And she gave a sigh. 'You have a mother, Mr Langdon?'

Hector said he had.

'Ah, she'll be worrying about you, I'm thinking.'

O'Hare broke in rather testily: 'Why should she? He's a man, is he not? He can look after himself.'

Mrs O'Hare looked crushed, bit her lip and said nothing.

'You'll be having a father too no doubt, Mr Langdon?' O'Hare said.

'Oh, yes. He's a solicitor.'

He wondered whether this would count in his favour or against him. It rather depended on what O'Hare's attitude to the tribe of lawyers happened to be.

But the man gave no indication either way. He said: 'You'll not have been in the War, I suppose? Too young for that.'

'I was too young, but I was in all the same. I added some years to my age and volunteered. I was in France with the infantry.'

Again he was not sure whether this would count for or against him. Noreen had shot a rather surprised glance at him when he made this revelation. He had never told her about his war service; had never felt the urge to.

'Ah!' O'Hare said. 'We have a hero amongst us, I see.'

Hector detected a sneer, but said nothing. He had a feeling that the visit was not going well and might get worse. He had begun to regret letting himself be persuaded to come. But it was too late for that now.

* * *

The arrival of Niall O'Hare was a welcome diversion, though the young man seemed no less wary of him than the parents. He repeated most of the questions that had already been asked and received the same answers. He was about the same age as Hector; black-haired, well-built and undeniably handsome. Hector wondered what he did for a living but decided not to ask.

Nobody mentioned the political situation. Mrs O'Hare had touched on the subject briefly and had promptly been put down by her husband, and after that there seemed to be a tacit agreement to avoid any reference to it.

Patrick was the next to arrive, and soon after that they had a meal in the dining-room, which was a long and rather bare chamber, a few degrees chillier than the one they had left. Conversation was spasmodic; it would flare up for a moment and then die away again. Patrick was the most talkative of the party. He was the youngest of the O'Hare family; nineteen years old and slightly built, with black hair like the others and rather delicate features. He was the only one who appeared to accept Hector as a welcome guest and not as some intruder who had gatecrashed his way in.

They were nearing the end of the meal when Sean walked in. He had not come to share the meal; having, he said, already eaten. He looked at Hector and said:

'So you're the Englishman.'

The words were spoken with no particular emphasis, but somehow to Hector it seemed as if they held a world of meaning in them. And the faint smile that went with them looked to him all too like the grin of a ravening wolf rather than the pleasant greeting of a prospective friend. He sensed hostility, not overt but only thinly hidden.

Sean was bigger than either of his brothers, and he looked strong. One could imagine him giving a good account of himself in a street fight or a pub brawl.

'Yes,' Hector said, 'I'm the Englishman.'

Sean was still looking hard at him, as if taking a mental imprint of the features, perhaps for future reference. Then he turned away without another word, walked to the head of the table where his father was sitting and said:

'I'd like a word with you, Da. Private.'

O'Hare looked surprised, but he stood up, and with a muttered word of apology left the room with his son. They were gone for about five minutes. When they came back O'Hare was looking grim, but he said nothing. Sean went up to Niall and whispered something in his ear. Niall stood up.

'Got to go now,' he said.

Mrs O'Hare looked at him in bewilderment. 'But why? And Sean only this minute arrived.'

Sean said: 'It's business, Ma.'

'At this time of night! What kind of business?'

'Never mind.'

'But — '

O'Hare broke in harshly: 'Let them go. Don't be making a fuss now.'

It silenced her. She just gave a bemused shake of the head and said no more.

Sean and Niall left the room, and there was an awkward silence. Hector wondered what was going on. It was obvious that something was, and he had an uneasy feeling that it boded no good for him. He thought Noreen looked puzzled and possibly a trifle worried. And that was none too reassuring.

Then Mrs O'Hare said: 'Why don't we all go back to the drawing-room? It's more comfortable there.'

No one raised any objection to this suggestion, so they did so. When they had made the move conversation was again of a faltering kind. The only person who seemed to be fully at ease was Patrick, and even he eventually appeared to feel the restraint that was affecting the others, and fell silent also.

'Well,' Hector said, after another of those awkward silences, 'I think it's time I was leaving. It's been a pleasure meeting you all.'

Nobody urged him to stay longer; not even Noreen. If her object had been for the visit to draw him into the bosom of her family, he felt that it had failed dismally. He could tell that he was not really welcome there; he was an intruder, an outsider. Whether in the course of time they would accept him was a question he could not answer. And perhaps it was one that never would be answered.

★　★　★

It was dark, with a hint of rain in the air, which was distinctly chilly, when he left; and he wished he had brought a coat. Only Noreen accompanied him to the door. She seemed to guess what was in his mind, and said:

'Don't be judging them from this first meeting. They need time to get used to you. It'll be better when you come again.'

He doubted it. He even wondered whether he would ever pay another visit to that gloomy house. He felt depressed when he kissed her goodnight; and as he walked away from the house the chill and the damp of the night did nothing to cheer him.

It was a pretty deserted street, and people were wise to stay indoors if there was nothing important to draw them out. A slight wind was springing up and doing nothing to make walking the streets a more attractive exercise. Hector could feel it getting through to his ribs, and he quickened his pace and could hear the sound of his own footsteps coming up from the pavement. There seemed to be no other sound but the soft keening of the wind and the distant murmur of traffic coming from the busier parts of the city.

He turned a corner and saw a small motor-van parked under a streetlamp some thirty yards ahead. Something warned him that here could be danger; it was a kind of sixth sense, and he checked his stride. But the warning had come too late. He heard the patter of feet behind him, and he began to turn. And this also was too late; he had scarcely begun the move when something was dropped over his head and shoulders, and the light was blotted out.

Judging by the odour of it, he guessed that it was a sack which had possibly been used for grain or meal, and before he could make any attempt to free himself from it, it was pulled down to his knees and a rope or cord was looped round it at waist height and drawn tight so that he could not move his arms.

He gave a cry, but it was muffled by the heavy sacking and he was half smothered by the mustiness inside his covering. Then he felt himself being hauled along the pavement, heels dragging; and a second or two later he was being bundled into what could only have been the back of the van. There followed the slamming of doors, and then the engine started and the whole van began to vibrate. There was a grinding of gears, and then it was on the move.

Hector, lying encased in the sack, could have shouted for help, but he knew that it would have been purposeless and decided not to waste his breath. No rescuer would have answered his cries even if they had been heard. His captors had spoken little, and never a word to him; they had allowed their actions to speak for them, and what these had told him was that he had been kidnapped. By whom or for what purpose he could only guess. And the result of this guessing was to depress his spirits to an even lower level than they had been for most of the evening.

★ ★ ★

It was not a long journey. Some ten minutes or so after being bundled into the van he was dragged out of it and stood up on his feet. He made no attempt to run away; he could not have seen where he was going and they would have recaptured him at once. So he allowed the men whoever they might be, to conduct him to wherever they would, making no resistance and saying nothing, simply waiting for events to unfold.

He was led away from the van, and it appeared as though they passed through a gateway and along a winding path until they came to a building of some sort. At least he supposed it was a building, for he heard the squeal of unoiled hinges as a door was opened, and he tripped over a threshold and might have fallen if one of the men had not grabbed the sack to hold him up. Then he heard the door closed behind him and knew they were inside because there was no longer the feel of any wind blowing.

He could tell that he was walking on a wooden floor, and he was guided across this for a few paces before being brought to a halt. Then there were some noises which he could not identify, and one of the men said:

'You'll be going down some stairs now, so watch yer step.'

He thought of asking how he was expected to watch his step when he could see nothing because of the sack covering him, but decided not to. And then they turned him round, and he went down backwards, with one of them leading the way and guiding his feet. He reached the bottom of the stairs, which seemed to be of stone or concrete, and heard a slamming noise overhead, which could have been a trapdoor closing. He was not greatly surprised, therefore, when the rope round his waist was untied and the sack lifted off, to discover that he was in a cellar.

Another thing that did not much surprise him was that two of his captors were already known to him. They were in fact Sean and Niall O'Hare. The third man, for there were but three, was somewhat older than either of them; a rough-looking character wearing a blue jersey under a rough tweed jacket. On his head he had a knitted woollen cap, also blue. He was carrying a hurricane lantern, which he must have picked up in the room above. It was the only light in the cellar, and it revealed a sanded floor, dirty white mildewed walls, a heap of mouldy straw in one corner and some wooden racks which might once have held bottles of wine but were now empty. The whole extent of the cellar was not more than twenty feet by fifteen.

Hector had a feeling that he might be there for some time. He was somewhat less than happy at the prospect.

13

Dungeon

He spoke to Sean. 'I suppose this was your idea. I thought something was afoot when you walked out on the party with Niall. But why?'

'As if you didn't know!' Sean spoke contemptuously. 'I recognized you soon as I set eyes on you. I'd seen you before. Only last time you were in uniform. You're a bloody Black-and-Tan. Isn't that the truth now? Deny it if you can.'

'I do deny it,' Hector said. But he knew it was useless. He was trying to think when and where Sean had seen him on duty; he had no recollection of seeing the man before that evening. But no doubt there were lots of people who had spotted him and made a note of his features on their memories for future reference. It was sheer bad luck that a brother of Noreen O'Hare should have been one of them. 'I don't know where you could have got such an idea.'

'Ye're a lyin' bastard,' the man in the blue jersey said. Later Hector was to learn that his name was Liam, but he never discovered what his surname was. 'There's too many of the likes of youse foulin' the streets o' Dublin with yer dirty feet.'

He hung the lantern on a hook in one of the beams supporting the floor above.

'Better search him,' Niall suggested.

'We're coming to it,' Sean said, rather snappishly, as if resentful of any advice coming from his younger brother. 'All in good time.'

He made the search himself. Hector remained passive, knowing that resistance would have been futile. Sean found nothing on him that might have linked him with the auxiliary police. Off duty he never carried anything of that description with him. There was no hidden weapon either.

'He's clean,' Sean said. He sounded faintly disappointed.

'So may I go now?' Hector asked.

It raised a laugh; but the laughter was not of the kind he would have liked to hear; it had a jeering quality.

'Looks like we got a joker here,' Liam said. 'But I'm thinkin' the joke's on him, sure it is.'

Without warning the man clenched his right fist and punched him on the jaw. The blow was delivered with an expertise that might have been acquired in the boxing ring, and it knocked him down on the hard floor. He was still lying there, half-stunned, when Sean gave him a kick in the ribs. Then Niall did the same, and Liam followed suit, demonstrating that he was as good with the toe as with the fist. After that they took it in turns to kick him. He tried to minimise the damage by curling up into a ball and holding his arms over his head to protect that vital part of his anatomy; but he was being given a lot of pain nevertheless, and it was a great relief when they finally stopped the kicking.

'Get up,' Sean said.

He was slow in doing so; he was not sure he could even manage it without aid. But he was given no time to find out. They hauled him to his feet and shoved him up against one of the walls, where he stood, teetering a little and feeling sore and groggy. When he breathed in he could feel the pain in his chest and wondered whether he had any broken ribs; but before he could give much thought to this possibility he was given something of even greater importance to think about.

This something was a revolver that had appeared in Liam's hand and must have been secreted somewhere about his person, maybe in one of the jacket pockets. This weapon was now pointing at the captive's head from a distance of no more than two feet.

Sean said: 'If you've any prayers to say, now's the time. Seeing as you're probably not a Catholic you'll not be needing a priest to administer the last rites.'

'So you're going to shoot me,' Hector said.

Oddly enough, he felt remarkably calm, even resigned. He knew that it would have been useless trying to escape; he would not have stood a chance. He might have begged for mercy, but he could not bring himself to do that; it would have been too cowardly. He refused to give them the satisfaction of seeing him grovelling before them. And besides, it would have served no purpose; they were not in the business of granting mercy.

'Is there any reason why we should not, will you tell me? Have you not shot enough of our people?'

'I suppose it wouldn't be any good telling you I haven't shot any of them?'

'And why would we be believing that? A man will tell any lie to save his skin.'

'Well, tell me this,' Hector said; playing for time, though he knew that they had all the time and however much they gave him, in the end it would come to the same thing. 'Are you the IRA?'

'Never mind who we are,' Sean said. 'What difference does it make to you? A bullet in the skull is just a bullet whoever 'tis that pulls the trigger of the gun.'

Which was the truth of course; and would it ease his passage into the next world, if there was a next one, to know to whom he was indebted for hastening his departure to that great unknown?

'Let's cut the gab an' get it over with,' Liam said.

He thumbed back the hammer of the revolver and his index finger was on the trigger.

'Wait!' Sean said.

Liam lowered the revolver and eased the hammer forward again. He looked at Sean, questioningly.

'It would be too easy for him,' Sean said. 'A quick death. All over. Just like that.' He snapped his fingers. 'Not good enough. We'll keep him on ice for a while. Leave him to think about it. Let him wonder when he's for the chop. Make him suffer for his crimes.'

'I have committed no crime,' Hector said. His voice was hoarse, and try as he might he could not control the shivering of his body. It was not from the chill in the cellar but from that step back at the brink of the abyss; the sudden unexpected reprieve. He had faced death and had been granted life, brief though the respite might be; and this was the reaction. He had not trembled when gazing into the muzzle of the gun, but now that it had been taken away the shakes had come. 'I am guilty of nothing. What are you accusing me of?'

'Ah, let's not go into that right now. Just the being here is enough. Just the wearing of that uniform, the black and the tan, sure it is.'

'But I've told you — '

'Oh, you've told us; I'm not denying that. But seeing is believing as they say, and I've seen you. With these two good eyes I've seen you in that damned livery, whatever you may say to the contrary.'

Hector gave up denying. Why bother to tell a lie when you knew it would not be believed? It was a waste of breath.

'We'll leave you now,' Sean said. 'But we'll be back. Don't be bothering to shout for help. Nobody will hear you. There's a bucket in that corner over there if you should feel the need of it. Sleep well, and pleasant dreams.'

They went then, taking the lantern with them. When they had shut the trapdoor he was left in complete darkness.

After a few minutes he groped his way to the steps and went up them until he could reach up and get his hands on the trapdoor. He tried to lift it, but without success. He climbed higher in order to get his shoulders under it and heave. The only result of this was the infliction of more pain on his ill-used body. He concluded that the trapdoor was either bolted or held down by some heavy weight. It was evident that he was not going to break out of his prison in that way. And what other way was there?

He retreated down the steps and made a tour of the cellar, feeling his way in the darkness. On one of the walls his fingers touched something smooth and slimy. He guessed that it was a slug creeping along that clammy surface, and he drew his hand back in disgust.

When he had completed this tour of his unpleasant quarters he sat down on the heap of straw and resigned himself to the situation. He was still shivering, and he burrowed into the straw, which, though it had a fusty odour, was reasonably dry and was certainly all the bedding he was going to have.

His body ached from the bruising it had sustained, and if he breathed in deeply he felt again the sharp pain in the chest from those possibly cracked ribs. He doubted whether he would sleep at all that night, and he lay there ruminating on the wretchedness of his plight and speculating in his mind on how long it would be before his captors decided to carry out the execution which had merely been postponed.

He had no idea what time it was when he did at last drop off to sleep, but when he woke he was surprised to find that the cellar was no longer completely dark. A very faint light was coming from a point low down on the opposite wall.

He thought of consulting his pocket watch to see what time it was, but then he remembered it had been taken from him, along with a packet of cigarettes and a box of matches, presumably to add this petty deprivation to the torture of his incarceration. When he moved he became aware of the stiffness in his limbs, and the movement also set two or three large rats scuttling away from the straw. He was so startled, and indeed revolted, by this evidence that he was sharing his dungeon with creatures he had always detested, that he gave a cry and started up from his rough bed.

But the animals had fled to some hole from which they had come, and he shook the straw from his clothing and walked to the place where the faint light was entering. He discovered that it was a cavity in the wall, about one foot square and a couple of feet from the floor. He stooped and peered into this opening, and saw that there was a brick-lined shaft leading up like a chimney to what must have been ground level, where an iron grating sealed it off. It was obviously a ventilation shaft, and it immediately occurred to him that here might be a way of escape.

Ignoring the extra pain inflicted by the exercise, he forced his way backwards into the narrow shaft and managed with difficulty to get far enough in to reach up to the grating. He had hoped that it would be loose like the cover of a drain, but in this he was to be disappointed; it was cemented into the brickwork and did not budge in the slightest when he put all the pressure on it of which he was capable.

His retreat from the shaft was even more difficult than the entering of it, and when he emerged at last it was at the cost of abrasions on both hands and not a little damage to his clothing.

He was cold, thirsty, hungry and frustrated. In this state he sat down on the straw with his back to the wall and waited for the next move on the part of his captors.

14

Big Occasion

It was Liam who came. He was accompanied by a young man whom Hector had not met before. Liam called him Mark, and he seemed quite a cheery character. Hector thought he had reason to be cheerful, seeing that he was not confined to a dungeon but was free to come and go as he pleased. In the present circumstances that seemed to him to be one of the greatest blessings on earth.

Liam had brought the lantern to augment what little light was coming in from the ventilation shaft, and Mark was carrying a biscuit tin and a can of water and an enamel mug. Liam had a revolver in one hand, just in case the prisoner should be inclined to try a bit of violence. In fact Hector had no such thought in his head. His mood was one of acute depression, and at the moment he was completely resigned to his fate.

'Well, now,' Liam said. 'How are we this bright and shiny morning?'

Hector answered gloomily: 'I don't know how you are, but if you're asking how I am, the answer is just what I imagine you'd expect. Bloody awful.'

Liam grinned in what appeared to Hector to be a particularly sadistic way and spoke to his companion.

'There's a thing now. No gratitude for a good night's lodging at no expense to himself, and us bringing breakfast to him and all. But that's the English for you; all take and no give. Isn't it the way it's been all down the years? Take what they can lay their grubby hands on in this dear country of ours and never give anything back.'

Mark seemed to be amused. Hector guessed that he was about the same age as himself and might have been expected to have some fellow feeling, but there was no indication of this. In the young man's eyes he could read only mockery.

'Take a good look at him, me boy,' Liam said. 'Because you won't get many more chances. He's got the sickness on him; the dying sickness. He'll not be much longer for this world, I'm thinking.'

'Is that a fact?' Mark said. 'Is that a fact now? And me thinking he looked in the best of health. But you never know, do you? You never know. Here today and gone tomorrow like the butterfly on the wing. A short life and a merry one.'

Hector saw that they were both at it, both mocking him. Well, if it pleased them to do it, let them. He refused to give them the satisfaction of reacting to their taunts.

When they had gone, taking the lantern with them, he looked in the tin and saw that it contained some dry biscuits and a slice of cheese. He breakfasted frugally on biscuit and cheese, washed down with cold water. In the days ahead the diet was to vary little; though now and then there was an apple, which he came to regard as a rare delicacy.

★   ★   ★

It was on the third day of his captivity that Noreen came to see him. She had been much in his mind, and he had wondered whether she was aware of what had happened to him; and if she was what her reaction had been. No doubt she would have been told that he was a Black-and-Tan.

She was accompanied by Sean and Liam. Patrick had never been there. Possibly the older brothers did not want him to be mixed up in the business.

It was Liam who came down the stairway first, carrying the lantern. Noreen followed him and Sean brought up the rear, closing the trapdoor behind him. Hector had been sitting on the straw, but he stood up when he heard the trapdoor opening.

The girl hesitated at the foot of the stairs while Liam hung up the lantern; and then she walked towards him slowly, halting a yard or so in front of him.

'Hello, Noreen,' he said; making no move.

She did not answer; she just stood there looking at him. He had not seen himself in a mirror since the day of his incarceration, but he could guess what he must look like: dirty, unshaven, haggard, his face bruised; not much like the smart young man she had taken to meet her family. And what an ill-fated visit that had turned out to be.

'I wondered when you would come. If you would come.'

'I am here now,' she said.

'You know what happened after I left you? They told you?'

'They told me everything,' she said; and she sounded bitter. 'Everything. You lied to me. You made a fool of me. I believed it all, and it was all lies.'

'No,' he said. 'Not all.'

'You said you were in Dublin to get material for a book. It wasn't true, was it?'

He gave a sigh. 'No, that wasn't true.'

'You're a dirty Black-and-Tan. Do you deny it?'

He sighed again. 'You wouldn't believe me if I did.'

'No,' she said. 'I've given up believing you.'

'I'm sorry,' he said. And was aware of the total inadequacy of the word.

She seized on it. 'Sorry! Is that all you can say? Do you think that excuses everything?' And then she took a step forward and slapped him on the cheek. 'I hate you! I hate you!'

The slap had stung, but he had not flinched. She turned away from him, and he could see tears falling. It was a sad end to something that had been so good; one hell of a sad end.

'Let's do it now,' Sean said.

Hector failed to grasp the significance of these words until he saw that the man had a black automatic pistol in his hand. Then it dawned on him.

'Now wait a minute,' he said.

But Liam had moved up swiftly behind him and put an arm lock on him. And then Sean was there in front, and he felt the cold metal of the gun touching his forehead. He had begun to struggle, but he stopped now, because struggling was useless. Sean had only to press the trigger and he would be a goner.

'This is it,' Sean said. 'This is where it all ends. For you.'

Hector had no doubt that he was speaking

the truth. They were tired of keeping him in the cellar, bringing him food, such as it was, having the bother of him on their hands. Now with just one bullet in the head this could all be brought to a conclusion.

He waited for the bullet, saying nothing, since there was nothing left to say. But the bullet never came, because the girl uttered one word.

'No!'

Sean looked at her, surprised, still holding the gun to Hector's forehead, waiting.

'You mustn't kill him. You mustn't. I won't let you.'

'But why? You hate him. You said so.'

'Yes, I do hate him for what he's done. But I still don't want him dead. I can't have that on my conscience.'

'But it won't be you that's doing the killing.'

'It makes no difference. I'd feel it just the same.'

'I believe it's still in love with the bastard, you are,' Sean said with disgust.

'No!' she said. 'No!' It was as though she were trying to convince herself. Or so it seemed to Hector.

'Then why?' Sean demanded.

'Oh, God!' she said. 'Does there have to be a reason? Has there not been enough of the killing? Must you have more blood on your hands? Must you?'

Sean seemed to hesitate, as if still inclined to finish the job. But then he lowered the gun and stowed it away. 'Well,' he said, 'we'll let him live for the present, just for the present. But I'll tell you this; his life's hanging by a thread, and any day the thread may be cut. That's the way it is and don't be forgetting it.'

They left after that. Halfway up the stairs Noreen cast one last glance back at Hector. There was regret in it, and perhaps accusation too; but he could detect no hatred; sorrow no doubt, but not that.

She did not come again.

★   ★   ★

He lost count of the days of his imprisonment. It had been early November when he had been taken to the cellar. Because of the chill he kept himself active, pacing back and forth in the confined space for hours on end, doing physical exercises, reciting bits of poetry to keep his brain from rusting, doing mental arithmetic, singing now and then.

He broke a length of wood off one of the bottle racks and used it to strike at the rats, but he never managed to kill one; they were too smart for him. Sometimes he thought of using the bludgeon to attack his captors when they came to visit him; and if they had ever come singly the plan might have been feasible; but there were always at least two of them, and one if not both would be armed, so that idea could be scrapped.

There was a permanent reek in the place. It had been bad enough at the start, but now there was the stench of the lavatory bucket adding its quota. The bucket was large, but it was gradually being filled, despite the fact that he was eating very little. His complaints about this were met with derision; it was evident that no one felt inclined to take on the job of sewage disposal. Perhaps they regarded this as part of his punishment.

He wondered when it would end, as it must eventually. But since he could anticipate only one probable way in which his imprisonment would terminate it was impossible for him to look forward to it with any degree of pleasure.

And then one day all four of them came together, the O'Hare brothers and Liam and Mark, and he guessed that something out of the ordinary was afoot. He guessed too that it would be nothing at all welcome to him.

'So,' he said, when they were all down in the cellar, 'what's the big occasion?'

Sean gave a laugh. 'As if you didn't know!'

This sounded ominous. And they had brought no food with them. Perhaps they knew they would not have to feed him any more.

'You're going to kill me now?'

None of them was showing a gun, but that did not mean there were not guns out of sight that could be brought into action if needed. Mark was carrying a bundle under his arm. Liam had the lantern.

Hector knew that it was dark outside, because no light was coming from the ventilator shaft. It figured that they would wish to do what they proposed doing by night rather than day. It was a deed for darkness.

Again Sean laughed. 'Are you so keen to have it done with? Can't you be waiting a little longer?'

'I can wait forever,' Hector said. 'Or at least for a lifetime.'

'But it's always a lifetime, is it not? Long or short, it's all you get.'

Liam was showing signs of impatience. 'Let's cut the cackle and be on our way.'

'Sure, sure. Let's have the sack, Mark.'

Hector saw now that what the young man had been holding under his arm was that very same sack in which he had been muffled when being brought to the cellar.

'You're going to put me in that thing again?' he asked.

'Just for a while. It won't be for long, I promise you.'

That again had an ominous ring to it. Nothing for him would last very long now. There was just this last piece of business to be seen to, and then it would all be finished.

He made no resistance when they slipped the sack over his head and shoulders. Where would have been the point? And once out of the cellar maybe there would be some faint hope of escape. He did not build much on it; he knew how slender it was. But it was like the drowning man's straw, to be clutched at with no real expectation that it would prove to be a life-saver.

He felt the cord slipped round his waist, and then they were guiding him to the stairway and he was going up the steps, stumbling now and then, but reaching the top and stepping out on to the wooden floor of the building he had never seen.

When they came out into the fresh cold air he could feel it through the sacking, and it was good to leave the reek of the dungeon behind, even though he might have so short a time left to enjoy the change. After this it was the reverse of the walk he had taken those few weeks ago that seemed an age. There was the winding pathway and the gate, and then the bundling into the back of the van. He could tell that two of the men had joined him there and knew that the others would be sitting in the front.

Again it was not a long journey. The van stopped; he was hauled out and marched away; nobody saying anything, not a word; and he saying nothing either, but just going blindly to his fate.

Suddenly they halted and the guiding hands were taken off him. This is it, he thought; this is the time when I start to run. For it's the last chance. But he did not run. Somehow, he just could not move. He stood there, waiting for the bullet in the brain; and it did not come. Instead, he heard the sound of footsteps retreating from him, fading into silence. And then the racket of the van starting up and driving away; and after that nothing else, nothing at all.

He was shaking. He could not believe it; could not believe that they had gone, that they had left him there, and that he was still alive. So for a while he did not even attempt to free himself from the sack. And when he did it was all so easy. The cord was loose, and he could get his hands out from under the sack and find the slipknot that was holding it. The cord fell away, and he wriggled out of the

132

sack and could really breathe the sweet air again; could suck in great mouthfuls of it and enjoy it as though it were a rare wine.

The place where he had been left was a narrow alleyway with blank walls on each side and only a faint light coming from a street-lamp at one end. He had no idea of where he was, but he was alive: that was the great, the almost unbelievable thing. He could not understand why; it was a complete mystery to him then; and he was content to leave it as such. He was alive and he was free; that was all that mattered.

Only later was he to learn something that almost certainly had a bearing on what had happened. He had lost track of time in the cellar, and did not know that the date of his being set free was the Seventh of December in the year 1921. He did not know either that on the previous day Michael Collins, as joint leader of an Irish delegation, had gone to Number Ten Downing Street for a meeting with the British Prime Minister, David Lloyd George.

This had been a momentous occasion when papers had been signed bringing into existence the Irish Free State. But it had also given rise to a divided Ireland, with all the troubles that this was to cause in times to come.

All this, however, was not to become known to Hector Langdon until later; and then he could only conclude that in the brief euphoria following this historic event his captors had decided that he had suffered enough and could be spared execution and set free. It was possible that Noreen had used what influence she had to help bring this about.

He was never to know where he had been held captive. He was never again to see the O'Hare boys or Mr and Mrs O'Hare or Liam or Mark. Most important of all, he was never to see Noreen again. His heart ached for her a little while, but not for long. His affair with her was just one more episode in his life. Like others, it had been good while it lasted, but it was not something to cause him any lasting regret.

As for Michael Collins, he had signed the treaty only under pressure, and was to lose his life in consequence; killed in a Republican ambush in August of the following year.

But by that time Hector was no longer a Black-and-Tan, and he had long since left Ireland, never to return.

15

New World

'And what do you propose to do now?' Arthur Langdon inquired.

Hector had a feeling that he had heard that question before. It always seemed to be cropping up whenever he was at home, and he never had an answer that was considered at all satisfactory by his father.

He was of course a disappointment to the old man; he knew that very well; he had never done anything that was right for him. First there had been the going off to war at an age when he should have stayed out of it; then there had been the disastrous riding school venture; and that had been followed by the Irish business, which too had been short-lived.

He had never given his parents a full account of what had happened in Dublin. The affair with Noreen O'Hare and all that had stemmed from it remained a secret. He knew it would have annoyed his father and distressed his mother; so there seemed to be no point in talking about it. The impression he tried to convey was that his tour of duty over there had all been a dull routine, more boring than dangerous.

Now, in answer to Arthur Langdon's question, he said: 'I think I'd like to go to America.'

'You mean emigrate?'

'Not necessarily. Just to take a look at the country; see what it has to offer for a man like me.'

'Hmph!' Arthur Langdon said; and it was obvious that he did not think very highly of the idea. 'Why should it have any more to offer than this country has?'

'It's the land of opportunity. People make fortunes there, become millionaires, that sort of thing.'

'And you think you could be one of them?'

'Anything is possible.'

'But not probable, I'd say.'

'Well, if I never go there I'll never know, shall I?'

'And how will you get there?'

'By the normal means, I suppose. Ship.'

'Well, of course.' Arthur Langdon spoke testily. 'I didn't imagine you proposed swimming. But steamship tickets cost money, and you'll need more when you get there. Have you got any?'

'Not a lot. I thought — '

'You thought I would finance you yet again. Is that it?'

Hector thought the 'yet again' was something of an exaggeration. It was his mother who had put up the money to invest in the riding school, and the Irish venture had cost his father nothing, so what did he have to complain about? It was just some more of the resentment coming out because his son had refused to go along with his wishes and take a deadly boring job in the solicitor's office.

'I did think you might give me a bit of help to get started. But of course if you won't — '

'Don't put words in my mouth. Did I say I wouldn't?'

'No, but — '

'I shall have to think it over. I can't say I like the idea, but when did my views ever count with you? However, if you're really serious about this — '

'Oh, I am, I am.'

'Well, we shall see. I fear no good will come of it. And your mother will not be happy about your going away again so soon. Nor I for that matter. We do think a lot of you, you know.'

Hector was surprised to hear his father make this admission. He had never given any strong indication that he had much paternal feeling for his son; but after all he was a dry, undemonstrative sort of man and tended to keep his feelings strictly bottled up. It was in his character.

★ ★ ★

Arthur Langdon was right about his wife's being unhappy about their son's proposal to go to America.

'It's so far away. Must you really go to such a distant country, Hector?'

'I feel I have to try it. It will be an adventure.'

'Yes, I suppose it will. And you were always such an adventurous boy.' She said this rather regretfully, as if she would have preferred him to have been somewhat more cautious, although that streak of recklessness in him might well have been inherited from her. Certainly it was unlikely to have come from Arthur. 'When do you propose going?'

'Soon. No sense in putting it off.'

'Well,' she said, 'I see that you've made up your mind. I don't suppose your father approves.'

Hector laughed. 'When has he ever approved of anything I've done?'

★ ★ ★

When it came to the point, Arthur Langdon paid for his passage to the United States and added a bit of capital to set him on his feet in the New World. His mother weighed in also with a useful sum, so that when he left the shores of his native land he was in better shape financially than a vast number of those Europeans who were flooding into the land of opportunity, hoping for a splendid future.

He was not himself going ostensibly as an immigrant. He would be a tourist with a British passport, and would not be called upon to spend time on Ellis Island being vetted by officials to determine whether he was fit to become a citizen of the United States of America. He was certainly not a member of the huddled masses yearning to breathe free.

It was in fact as a passenger in the tourist class on board the *Aquitania* that he sailed in the spring of 1922, and arrived in New York full of hope and great expectations. The Statue of Liberty and the skyscrapers of Manhattan Island seemed to beckon to him when he stood on the deck of the great liner as she moved towards the pier where he was to disembark. Excitement bubbled up in him as he had his first glimpse of this gateway to that golden land where he hoped to make his fortune.

Later a certain amount of disillusionment was to set in. He soon came to realize that he had been altogether too sanguine regarding his prospects in this brave new world. With little capital and no readily marketable skills, he could find no one eager to snap up his services and pay a generous salary for the privilege of employing him. The plain and disagreeable fact was that no one wanted him at all.

He could perhaps have found an unskilled labouring job, but in this he would have been competing with numberless immigrants from the Old World who were only too eager to take any kind of employment, even of the most menial description, in order to get a foot on the ladder. To him such a way of starting was not acceptable; he had not come so far to wield a pick and shovel; that was not his idea at all. Indeed, his plans regarding what he would do when he reached America had been so vague as to be virtually non-existent; he had been so naïve as to believe that opportunities for making himself rich would drop into his lap as if by some divine dispensation. By the end of his second week in New York he was forced to the conclusion that this was very far from being the case.

He had been living in a modest hotel, and the only incident of any note that occurred during those first two weeks took place as he was walking down Fifth Avenue one morning. Suddenly he heard pistol shots, and a moment later two men rushed out of a jeweller's shop with guns in their hands. One was carrying a canvas holdall, and both of them jumped into a car that was waiting by the kerb with the engine running and a third man at the wheel.

It started moving off immediately, just as another man came staggering out of the shop, bleeding from a wound in his left arm. The blood had soaked into his sleeve and was dripping off the tips of his fingers. But he seemed to be a tough individual, for in spite of his injury he opened fire on the getaway vehicle with a black automatic which he had in his right hand. He was not at all bad with the gun either, and he scored a hit on one of the rear tyres, which went flat straightaway. And at that moment a police car appeared on the scene and began chasing the robbers' car, which was proceeding somewhat erratically because of the flat tyre at the back.

So now there were policemen leaning out of the pursuing vehicle and firing pistols at the other one, and crooks shooting back at them with everything they had. Bullets were flying everywhere and pedestrians were running for cover to avoid being caught in the crossfire, while other cars were riding up on to the sidewalks and crashing into one another, or even into shop windows; so that, what with one thing and another, it was really quite a chaotic scene in downtown New York for a while.

To Hector all this came as no surprise. It was just the sort of thing he had expected, and he would have been amazed and not a little disappointed if he had failed to come across the kind of mayhem he had so often seen portrayed on the cinema screen back home in England. After all, was not America the notorious land of the gangster and the gunman? So surely running battles between criminals and armed police were commonplace on the streets.

Mentioning this to a chance acquaintance in a bar, he was informed that it was a misconception. The man had lived in New York all his life and had never seen a shot fired by a cop or a robber. But Hector, having been there for only a few days and chancing to be on the scene of one such occurrence, had jumped to the conclusion that there was continual armed warfare between officer and criminal. From this it was but a step to believing that in such a violent country he was as much in danger of stopping a stray bullet as he had been in Dublin.

He decided, therefore, to obtain for himself the means of personal defence; namely, a gun. And as matters turned out it was to prove the most fateful decision he had ever taken.

He had no difficulty in getting the weapon. He simply had to walk into a gun store and pick up what he wanted. The choice was wide, and the only problem was in making up his mind which of the many varieties of handgun to buy. In the end he settled for a Colt .38 calibre revolver with a four-inch-long barrel, which the salesman assured him was a very nice gun, and one that he could particularly recommend. Hector also bought two boxes of ammunition, and left the store feeling that he had made himself rather more secure in what he regarded as a pretty lawless country.

Soon after he had bought the revolver he decided to leave New York. He remembered a piece of advice often given to those seeking their fortune in North America. It was: 'Go west, young man'.

He thought he could do no better than take that advice. He packed his bags and headed for the Grand Central Railroad Station.

16

Stranger in Town

As things turned out, he did not immediately travel so much west as south, moving from town to town and viewing the country from the windows of rail-cars. Thus it was that by a quirk of fate he found himself one day in Nashville, Tennessee. And it was in the lounge of a rather seedy hotel that he fell in with a character named Ephraim Snitzler.

Snitzler was a smallish, wiry man, maybe forty years old or so, and wearing a brown check suit and a string tie. He had a bony face, pale blue eyes and hair like bleached tow. He also had a pointed beard, very large ears and a prominent nose. Hector thought there was a gnomish look about him; but he was a very friendly gnome, and the two of them took to each other from the start.

It was not long before Snitzler volunteered the information that he was in Nashville to pick up a fresh supply of his stock-in-trade, which had run somewhat low.

'And what would this stock-in-trade be?' Hector asked.

'Bibles chiefly,' Snitzler said.

'Bibles! You're telling me you sell Bibles?'

'And tracts. Does that surprise you?'

'It does a little,' Hector admitted. He would not have put Snitzler down as a Bible salesman. He did not look the part. But if it came to that, what did a Bible salesman look like? Was there any instantly recognizable feature that marked him out from the common run of men? Why should not Snitzler make his living selling Bibles as well as the next man? 'It's not quite what I'd have expected, that's all.'

'And yet,' Snitzler said, 'you should know this is plumb in the heart of the Bible belt; so where better to find a ready market for the Good Book?'

Hector could see that there was logic in this, though it was the first time he had ever heard of the Bible belt. Snitzler explained that this was the area of southern United States where the people were predominantly fundamentalist and puritanical Christian.

'And you?' Hector asked.

Snitzler grinned and gave a wink. 'Me, I'm just the guy who supplies the mental fodder.'

Hector gathered that there was nothing fundamental or puritanical about his own faith. And maybe if it came to the point, not a lot of the Christian either.

'So how about you?' Snitzler asked. 'What's your line of business?'

Hector was forced to admit that he had no particular line. 'Fact is I'm on my way out west to make my fortune.'

Even as he said it, he felt that it sounded crazy; and he could tell that Snitzler thought so too. He gave a shake of the head.

'That gold rush ended long ago. The old song may say there's lots of gold on the banks of Sacramento, but it ain't true any more. It's all stashed away in a different kinda bank, or in Fort Knox. I guess back in England things out here looked a darn sight rosier than they really are. Dollar bills don't grow on trees even in California. Still, you may make it big. Don't let me discourage you.'

Hector thought this a bit rich, coming from a man who had already made a pretty good fist of doing just that. Snitzler himself may have realized this; for as if to introduce a more cheerful note, he said:

'Look, Hector, I'll be travelling west soon's I've stocked up. Why don't you come along for the ride? I'd be glad of the company, and I've taken a real shine to you. What you say?'

It was an offer that required no protracted thinking about. Hector's purse was beginning to feel much too light for comfort, and the

146

chance of some free transportation was too good to miss.

'I'd be much obliged.'

★ ★ ★

Snitzler had not revealed what form the transport would take, and Hector had not liked to ask. It turned out to be a Model T Ford van. Snitzler and Hector rode in the front, and the trade goods were loaded into the back. They left Nashville the next day, as soon as the stock had been picked up.

Snitzler drove, but he said that Hector could take a turn at the wheel now and then to give him a break. Hector pointed out that, though he had ridden a motor-bike, he had never driven a car. Snitzler said this was no problem, and here was his chance to learn.

'It's plumb easy. I'll teach you. You'll pick it up in no time at all.'

The van was painted a bilious yellow, and it was a genuine tin lizzie. It shook and rattled its way along the highways and byways of that part of America which Snitzler regarded as his market.

'It's a great life, Hector,' he said. 'It's the variety, you see. You never know what's going to happen from one day to the next.'

As he had forecast, Hector soon got the

147

hang of driving the van and was able to take his turn at the wheel. Snitzler also outlined to him the technique of door-to-door salesmanship in the small towns and country districts where he operated. It was a maxim of his that you should try if possible to avoid calling at a house when the man was at home. Women were the real customers, because besides the Bibles and tracts he had other goods to sell, which he would bring out if he judged he had a likely buyer. These were ointments and lotions guaranteed to remove wrinkles and magically restore that youthful look.

'They're not all as puritanical as you might think. Most of 'em are just longing for that elixir that'll make them young and beautiful again; even though most never had any beauty to speak of anyway.'

One day he suggested that Hector should try his hand at the selling game.

'A young good-looking guy like you couldn't go wrong. Just turn on the charm, and before you know where you are you'll have them falling over themselves to invite you in and buy whatever you have to sell. If only I was your age and looked like you! They'll be eating out of your hand. It'll be a cinch.'

And he was right.

Hector was nervous at first when he walked

up to a door with the suitcase of trade goods in his hand. But he soon gained confidence when he found how easy it was to sell to these women. There were exceptions of course; some were real battle-axes who would have nothing to do with him and slammed the door in his face. But on the whole he did very well and even came to enjoy the game.

Snitzler was pleased. 'Boy, if only I had your looks! I'd be a millionaire.'

★ ★ ★

He was not exclusively a door-to-door salesman. He had a folding table in the van, and he would set this up at different places and lay out his wares on this improvised stall. He had a real huckster's spiel and would soon draw a crowd. He was in the direct line of descent from the old-time purveyors of snake-oil, which was reputed, by the salesmen at least, to cure practically all the ailments known to mankind. Snitzler's pills and potions were rather more sophisticated, but no more effective. As of old, it was essential for the vendor to be well on his way before the buyer could discover that he had been gulled and maybe feel resentful enough to come looking for the deceiver with a gun.

One of his most popular lines was a

guaranteed hair-restorer made to a secret formula known only to himself.

'It always gets the guys with the hair problems, and there's plenty of them. They'll try anything in the hope of getting the stuff to grow again.'

'And what's in it?' Hector asked.

Snitzler grinned. 'Horse liniment mainly. Makes the scalp tingle so they think it must be working. Like the guy said, there's one born every minute.'

He had set up his stall one day in a little one-horse town in Arkansas and was pushing this stuff for all he was worth to a small gathering of interested townsfolk while Hector stood by admiring his technique. The bottles had printed labels on them which read: 'Lightning Hair Restorer. New Growth Guaranteed. Money Refunded If Not Fully Effective.'

Hector once asked him if he had ever been called upon to refund any money.

Snitzler grinned. 'It's a big country. I'm never in the same place twice. I keep on the move.'

'One jump ahead of the suckers?'

'That's about it.'

As proof of the efficacy of the hair restorer he set up a large head and shoulders photograph of himself with a completely bald head, and below it the inscription: 'Before Using Lightning.' There was a second photograph as he now was with a mass of hair as thick as a doormat. This was captioned: 'Three Months After Use'.

Hector asked him how he managed to get the bald effect.

'Simplest thing in the world,' Snitzler said. 'Had my head shaved. Took a while to grow again, but it was worth it. Great advertisement for the restorer.'

'Which of course you used on yourself.'

'Now there's a funny thing,' Snitzler said. 'Just one drop of that stuff and my hair grew like crazy.'

Hector laughed. 'Well, who would believe it!'

'You'd be surprised,' Snitzler said. 'You'd be surprised.'

On this occasion, however, it was he himself who was in for a surprise; and a nasty one at that. He was busy giving his salesman's spiel to the little crowd in front of the stall when he was interrupted by someone shouting:

'You're nothing but a goddamn shyster!'

It stopped Snitzler in mid-flow. Hector had never seen him so disconcerted. For a moment he was struck dumb; which was a rare occurrence for him.

The man who had made the accusation now elbowed his way to the front of the gathering and was revealed as a coarse-looking bulky character wearing Levis and a corduroy jacket and a Stetson hat. He looked angry. Hector thought he also looked highly dangerous.

Snitzler, taken out of his stride but quickly regaining his composure, said: 'I don't think I can have heard you correctly, sir.'

'You heard me,' the man said. 'And you know me, don't you?'

'I can't say that I do. Have we met?'

'Durn right, we have. A year ago.'

'I don't recall — '

'Maybe you don't. But I do. It was in a little place called Dansville in Tennessee. You set your stall up there an' sold me a bottle of hair restorer. Two dollars I paid for it, like you're charging now.'

'Ah!' Snitzler said. And he was beginning to look somewhat uneasy. 'Now I do have some recollection. The face, sir, is familiar.'

Hector thought he had reason to feel anxious. The situation that he tried to avoid by constantly changing his itinerary and never visiting the same place twice had come about despite every precaution. A former customer had perhaps changed his abode, and their paths had crossed. It was a danger

152

that could never be entirely eliminated.

'And was the result, sir, not entirely to your satisfaction?' Snitzler inquired.

'Not to my satisfaction!' The bulky man had gone red in the face with anger. 'Does this look like satisfaction?'

He whipped off the Stetson hat and revealed a head which, apart from a sparse fringe around the lower regions had no more hair on it than might have been found on a billiard ball. The bald dome gleamed in the afternoon sunlight.

A titter went up from the crowd, which seemed to enrage the bulky man even more. He scowled at Snitzler.

'What have you got to say for yourself, you two-bit chiseller?'

'Perhaps,' Snitzler suggested, 'you failed to persevere with the treatment. Yours looks like a difficult case. Why not try another bottle or two?'

The man rammed his hat back on. 'Difficult case be damned! It's a swindle, that's what it is. The stuff's no use and you know it.'

'But that's just not true. There's the proof.' Snitzler pointed at the photographs. 'The camera cannot lie.'

And that, Hector thought, was a lie in itself. But he said nothing. He waited with some trepidation for further developments. The crowd seemed to be waiting expectantly too. And there was not long to wait.

'You're wearing a wig; that's what it is,' the bulky man said. 'You're still bald, but you've got a wig to cover it up.'

He stepped forward and knocked Snitzler down with a stiff right hook to the jaw. Then, while Snitzler was still lying rather dazed in the dust, he grabbed a handful of the victim's abundant hair and gave it a vicious tug. Snitzler let out a howl of anguish, but his assailant, still trying to prove that the hair was a wig, continued to pull at it and succeeded only in dragging the hapless salesman along the ground.

Hector decided that enough was enough and it was time to take a hand in the game. So he stepped up to the bulky man and grabbed his arm.

'Hold it!'

The man let go of Snitzler's hair and took a swing at this new target. Hector dodged the blow and punched the man in the gut. His fist sank in as if it had struck a large boiled pudding, and the man gave a gasp as the air was driven out of him. Hector took the opportunity to haul Snitzler to his feet; but the bulky man was not out of action for long. He gave a growl and took another swipe at

Hector, who was again nimble enough to avoid the punch without much trouble. In return he sank his fist again into the bulging paunch.

And now the crowd, fickle as all crowds were, was turning against the bulky man. Apparently he was a stranger in town, and strangers are always suspect. Moreover, he had made an accusation about Snitzler's hair that had been proved utterly false. Sympathy had switched to the purveyor of miracle cures, and his adversary was soon being jostled and derided by the natives. Seeing which way the wind was blowing, he decided to call it a day and slunk off, with jeers and catcalls speeding him on his way.

But Snitzler had also had enough. He started packing the gear back in the van, with Hector lending a hand. There seemed to be some disappointment in the crowd; and having seen the bulky man off, they seemed to think they had a right to some further attention from the mountebank.

Snitzler ignored them. He climbed into the driving seat and Hector swung the starting handle. The van began to shudder and creep forward as it always did, and Hector ran round to the side and got in beside the driver. In a moment they were away, leaving a number of possible customers feeling most disgruntled behind them.

'That was an unfortunate occurrence,' Hector said. 'Might have done some good business if that man hadn't turned up.'

'Occupational hazard,' Snitzler said.

'Has anything like it happened before?'

'Once or twice. You do your best to avoid such mishaps, but you can never be sure some guy you've had dealings with someplace else won't pop up out of the blue and cut up rough. And people can be so upset when they think they've been conned.'

'With reason, wouldn't you say?'

'Well, maybe. But they ask for it, don't they? They do ask for it.'

'How's the jaw?'

Snitzler moved it around a bit to see if it was still in working order, and apparently it was.

'It'll do. Thanks for the help. You're pretty handy with the mitts. I guess you've had experience.'

'Some,' Hector said.

17

Importunate Widow

They were near a little place called
Ramworth when Hector ran into a spot of
trouble. They had worked their way westward
almost to the border between Arkansas and
Texas at the time, and they were moving into
the countryside just outside the town when
they came to a wooden bungalow with a few
acres of land that seemed to go with it.

It was pretty isolated and stood well back
from the hard road at the end of a dusty
track. There were outhouses, all somewhat
dilapidated, and a few items of farm
machinery standing here and there, which
appeared to indicate that something had been
going on in the agricultural line, though no
such activity was observable at the moment.
Nothing gave any indication of much
prosperity, let alone wealth, but Snitzler
thought it might be worth a visit, and he
suggested that Hector should go and take a
look at things while he stayed in the van.

So Hector took the suitcase of trade goods
and walked down the track towards the

dwelling. There was a front porch with a couple of steps leading up to it, and a front door in need of a fresh coat of paint and an old rocking-chair at one side.

He rapped on the door with his knuckles, and after a while it was opened by a plump blonde, maybe pushing forty and not at all bad-looking in a full-blown sort of way.

'Good afternoon,' Hector said. 'I wonder whether you would be interested in buying a Bible.'

It seemed unlikely. He had seldom seen anyone who appeared less likely to be looking for a Bible; but you never knew. At least she was not slamming the door in his face or telling him to get to hell out of it.

'So,' she said, 'you're selling Bibles, are you?' She sounded faintly amused, as if she thought it was something of a joke.

'Amongst other things.'

'What other things?'

'Toiletry. This and that.'

He had set the suitcase down but had made no attempt to open it. It was a hot day, and though he was in shirtsleeves he was sweating a little. He could see no sign of any man about the place, or indeed of anyone but the woman.

She said. 'I guess you better come inside and show me what you got.'

She stood back from the door, and he picked up the suitcase and went in. There was an entrance hall which was also a passage, and she ushered him into a room opening off to the left. It was a sitting-room and it contained some well-worn armchairs and a sofa and an upright piano. Standing on the piano was a large framed photograph of a man with close-set eyes and a horseshoe moustache. It was the first thing that caught his eye, and the woman must have noticed him looking at it, for she said:

'That's my husband, Zeke. I'm Mrs Wayburn, Leila, if you want to know.'

He was not sure that he did, but he said: 'Is that so? He's a handsome man, your husband.' Which was a lie; he had never seen a more mean-looking face.

'Was,' she said. 'He died last week.'

'Oh dear! I'm sorry to hear that. You must miss him.'

'Like I'd miss a hole in the head. He was a skunk. Best thing ever happened to me, day he up an' died. All this is mine now, and no damned man to tell me what I can or cannot do.'

'But you still keep his picture up there. Why?'

'So's I can gloat. He's there lookin' on but he can't touch me.'

Hector was at a loss what to say to this, so he said nothing.

'Fishbone done it,' the woman said. 'Choked him. Glad I give him that fish. Never know, do you?'

She was wearing a flowered cotton dress, and it was stretched tightly over her ample figure. It was even hotter in the room than it had been outside, and when she had seated Hector in one of the armchairs she suggested he might like something to lubricate his throat.

'I sure know I could use a drink,' she said. And without waiting for an answer from him she went out of the room and came back with an unlabelled bottle, two glasses and a jug of iced water on a tray. She set this down on a side-table, poured the drinks and handed one to Hector. He drank some of the liquid, which had to be as illegal as hell under the Prohibition laws, and it seemed to take the lining off his throat. She took a swig of the stuff herself and said: 'You didn't tell me your name.'

He told her, and took another cautious pull at the hooch, which brought tears to his eyes and started a fire down below.

'So where you from?'

'England.'

'Oh, sure, I shoulda guessed, the way you

160

talk. So what you doin' down here sellin' Bibles?'

'Selling Bibles,' Hector said.

She gave a laugh, and he was thinking she really did seem to be enjoying her freedom from the lately deceased skunk. That and the moonshine.

'Well, now to business,' he said.

He set his glass down and reached towards the suitcase; but before he could open it she said: 'Wait! Just stay here a minute and don't run away.'

She went out of the room then, but left the door open. Thus forced to postpone the sales talk, Hector sat back in the chair and drank some more of the hooch. A minute or two passed; and then he heard her calling to him.

'Come here a moment, Hector, I've something interesting to show you.'

He got up and went into the passageway.

'Where are you?' he asked.

'In here. Do hurry.'

The voice was coming from a little way along the passage, where another door was standing open. He walked to the doorway and looked into what was obviously a bedroom, but he could see nothing of the woman; so he went in. She was standing on the left, and he saw that she had taken off the flowered dress and was now in a loose kimono, black, with a

161

golden dragon motif.

He knew then that he ought to get out of there in double-quick time; but he did not move. He said:

'So what is it you have to show me?'

'Why, this,' she said. And she released the sash and opened the kimono. 'Do you like it?'

There was plenty of it; that was certain. In a way, the sheer quantity of it was fascinating.

'Very nice,' he said. 'Yes, very nice. But now it's getting late and I really must go.'

He began to retreat, but she was too quick for him. She was nearer to the door than he was, and she slammed it shut and stood between him and it. To open it he would have had to manhandle her out of the way, and this he hesitated to do.

'Now look,' he said. 'This is crazy. What do you want from me?'

'Well,' she said, 'if that ain't the stupidest damn question ever was! What do you think I want? I want a bit of lovin', that's what. Ain't too much to ask, is it?'

'Maybe it is at that.'

'Aw, come on, Hec,' she said. 'Why don't you peel off them clo's? Sure is hot 'nuff.'

'No,' he said. 'I don't think that would be wise.'

'Wise or not, thing is you don't have no choice.'

She dipped a hand into a pocket of the kimono and hauled out a little nickel-plated pistol, which she pointed at his stomach.

'See what I mean?'

He wished then that he had brought his own gun, which was stowed away in his luggage in the van. But it had never entered his mind that he might have need of it.

'Now,' he said, 'be careful with that thing. It could go off and hurt someone.'

She gave a laugh. 'Damn right it could. Make a nasty little hole in your gut if it did. So be sensible. Get them clo's off an enjoy yourself. Ain't askin' much, is it?'

He gave a shrug. 'Well, maybe not.'

'Now you're being sensible.'

She stood between him and the door, watching him as he undressed; and when he was ready she let the kimono drop to the floor, but kept the gun in her hand. She walked over to the bed and climbed on to it, making the mattress creak under her weight. Hector thought of making a grab at the gun, but it would have been a risky thing to do; and why bother? Why not take the easy way?

It was like making love to a semi-inflated air-bed. The flesh seemed to envelop him in warm folds. The woman was giving little cries of delight: 'Oh boy! Oh boy! Oh boy!' He heard the gun fall from her hand to the floor.

He was thankful there were no neighbours to listen in. The window was open and the curtains were not drawn, but there was no one outside to watch the proceedings and no skunk to come walking in. He was somewhere else, pushing up daisies.

* * *

When he was dressed she gave him a cigarette and lit one for herself. She was wearing the kimono again and looked happy. They went to the sitting-room and this time he did manage to get the suitcase open. So they sat there, smoking and drinking more of the hooch, while she picked out things from the merchandise that she felt she would like to buy.

She paid him before he left, and gave him a big wet parting kiss.

'Ever come this way again, don't hesitate to call in. Maybe I buy a Bible next time.' She laughed, and her breasts wobbled with the laughter, 'Cheap at the price. You betcha.'

* * *

He found Snitzler asleep in the cab of the van when he got back to it. Snitzler woke up and said:

'You took a hell of a time. What kept you?'

'The woman.'

Snitzler grinned. 'I just wish I had what you got, Hector. It ain't fair.'

'She said if I was ever this way again to call in and she'd buy a Bible. She's a widow woman. Used to be married to a skunk called Ezekial Wayburn. He died last week, choked on a fishbone. She wishes she'd fed him fish more often.'

'Sounds like a real nice God-fearing lady,' Snitzler said. 'Crank her up, boy, and let's be on our way.'

Hector cranked her up and jumped in beside the driver. Snitzler got the tin lizzie going, and they left the importunate widow Wayburn to her cosmetics and her memories.

18

Cattle Ranch

Three days later Hector decided it was time to quit the business. He had found his travels with Snitzler both interesting and enjoyable, but now the time had come to move on. Snitzler had come as far west as he intended and would be returning to Nashville by a different route, taking in places he had never visited before and where he hoped he would be unrecognized by any disgruntled former customer. This did not fit in with Hector's plans, and he said so.

Snitzler was not surprised, since he had known from the start that Hector had come with him just for the ride.

'Be sorry to lose you all the same. Sure you won't change your mind, stick with it? I can use a partner, and you been getting the hang of things mighty quick.'

Hector admitted that the idea had a certain appeal. 'You've been a good pal, Ephraim, and we've got on well together. But you'd need to double your turnover to make it financially viable, and I don't see how that would be possible.'

'Maybe you're right at that.'

'And besides, it's not really something I could stick at for long. In the end we'd be bound to split up. Best to do it now while we're still on good terms.'

'Right again, I guess,' Snitzler said. 'Just remains to wish you luck and the best of fortune. And to help you on your way here's a little something for the pocket.'

The little something was fifty dollars in cash. Hector protested that he could not accept so much, seeing that it was he who was indebted to Snitzler for helping him on his way. Snitzler said that was just crap and he had earned the money. So finally Hector stopped protesting and took the dollars. He might soon need them.

They shook hands at parting, and the last Hector ever saw of the Bible and quack medicine merchant was of him climbing into the cab of the Ford van and driving away in a cloud of dust.

★ ★ ★

He was on his own again, and he was in Texas, the Lone Star State. For him it had always had a romantic appeal because it figured in so many stories about the Wild

167

West that he had read and in films he had seen. He knew that those days had long gone by, but surely some of the romance must have endured.

He set out to find it, travelling from place to place, sometimes by bus, more often by hitch-hiking in cars and lorries. In this way he covered quite a large area of the state, but he was still without a job and the money was dribbling away. The wide horizons were all very well, but they did not feed you or pay for hotel rooms in small towns.

The situation was not yet desperate, but it was certainly heading that way when he had a lucky break. He was on the road with a big duffel-bag which now contained all his gear, the suitcases having been discarded as less practical some time back, when he flagged down a big Chrysler tourer. There was just one person in the car, a man of about thirty-five, fair-haired, broad-shouldered, with a tanned, weatherbeaten face. He leaned out of the car and said:

'Where you heading, son?'

'Wherever you are,' Hector said.

'Like that, is it? Well, hop in.'

Hector dumped his bag in the back and got in beside the big man, who immediately set the car in motion again.

'On the road, huh?'

'For the present, yes.'

'What's your name?'

Hector told him.

'And English I'd guess.'

'That's so.'

'I'm Jed Johnson. What you doing in this neck of the woods?'

'Seeking my fortune,' Hector said.

Johnson laughed. 'Think you'll find it here?'

'I'm beginning to have doubts.'

'So the going's tough, is it? Got any qualifications?'

'Nothing to speak of.' He wondered whether to tell Johnson he could sell Bibles, but decided not to. 'I know how to fire a rifle and throw a grenade, but there doesn't seem to be much call for that now.'

Johnson seemed interested. 'Rifles and grenades! So you were in the war?'

'Yes.'

'In France?'

'Yes.'

'Me too,' Johnson said. 'Hi, buddie!'

Soon he was confiding in Hector like a long lost friend in that easy way Americans had. It transpired that he had been a captain in the United States Expeditionary Force and had fought on the Western Front. Soon after the end of the war an uncle had died and left him a cattle ranch in Texas. So he decided to quit the army and take up ranching.

'Look, Hector,' he said. 'If you got nothing better to do, why don't you come back with me and spend some time on the ranch? How does that sound to you?'

To Hector it sounded fine. He could not have asked for anything better than the opportunity to live for a time on a genuine Texas cattle ranch. The prospect excited him, and he accepted the invitation without hesitation.

'I'd love it.'

A couple of miles or so further on a dirt road branched off to the right. Johnson steered the Chrysler on to it, and about another mile of this rough track brought them to the ranch house and a lot of outbuildings.

'This is it,' Johnson said.

There was a wooden arch supporting a signboard on which were painted the words: Circle T Ranch; and above this inscription was the brand mark — a capital T enclosed by a circle. Surmounting the signboard was a pair of bull's horns.

Johnson drove the Chrysler under the arch and stopped it at the front of the house. It was a big building, almost palatial in scale. It was all white and was built in the Spanish style, with a portico along the front and tall windows. Hector was impressed. Anyone living in a house like that surely had to have no lack of money.

'Come inside,' Johnson said.

They went up on to the portico and in through the wide front doorway. There was a spacious entrance hall with an impressive staircase curving up to a gallery. The floor was wood-block, gleaming darkly with polish.

As they entered a woman came into the hall; black-haired, attractive, probably younger than Johnson by quite a few years.

'Ah!' she said. 'So you're back. I thought I heard the car. And I see you've brought someone with you.'

Johnson hastened to make the introduction. 'My dear, this is Hector Langdon. Hector, my wife Paula.'

'Well, hello there, Hector,' she said; and he thought for a moment she was going to offer her hand, but she did not, perhaps because she had noticed how grubby his was.

She was very elegantly dressed and looked cool. She made him feel like a tramp in contrast; travel-stained, sweaty, unshaven and rather dirty. She might have been asking herself where on earth her husband had picked up this piece of garbage. And yet he detected a hint of amusement in her eye and no evidence of any aversion.

Johnson said: 'Hector and I were buddies over there.'

'You knew each other?'

She was still looking at Hector, and seemed to be addressing the question to him.

He said: 'Not exactly. I was in the British army. Mr Johnson of course was with the Americans. We never actually met.'

'It was the same war,' Johnson said. 'And let's have none of that Mister nonsense. Call me Jed. We don't stand on ceremony here.'

'And what are you doing in Texas, Hector?' Paula asked.

It was Johnson who answered: 'Looking to make his fortune.'

She smiled. 'And with what results?' Still looking at Hector.

'Very little so far, I'm afraid.'

'I invited him to stay with us for a time,' Johnson said.

Hector put in quickly: 'If that's all right with you, Mrs Johnson. I don't want to impose on your hospitality.'

'Oh it'll be no imposition,' she said. 'We have plenty of room. And you may call me Paula, you know. Like Jed told you; no ceremony in this house.'

★ ★ ★

The room allotted to him was just about the biggest he had ever slept in. There was a bathroom attached, and the first thing he did was take a bath and shave and generally spruce himself up. There was not much he could do about the clothes except brush them, but fortunately he had a clean shirt, somewhat creased from being in the duffel-bag but not too badly, so that when he went down to dinner he felt more presentable than he had been when he walked into the house.

There were two other people besides the Johnsons at the long dining-table. The man was a cousin of Johnson's named Rory Milligan; a rather stumpy individual with a rosy face and a drooping moustache. He was about the same age as Johnson, but his hair was receding from a broad, shiny forehead. His wife, Molly, was a fluffy blonde, pretty in a doll-like way, and more high-spirited than the man. While he seemed inclined to moroseness, she was a chatterer and had a giggling laugh which broke out on the smallest encouragement.

It seemed to Hector that Rory found her chatter and laughter an irritation, and on one occasion he snapped at her: 'For God's sake, Moll, give it a rest.'

It disconcerted her, but only for while, and very soon she was at it again. Hector found himself the target of much of her chatter, and he had to field a lot of questions of a personal nature; but he was not bothered. The fluffy blonde rather amused him.

He imagined at first that the Milligans were simply at the ranch on a visit, but he discovered later that they were a fixture. Rory earned his keep by doing the accounts and any other paperwork connected with the business. Johnson confessed that this side of the enterprise was not his line; he preferred the great outdoors.

Hector got the impression that Milligan was not altogether happy in his situation as an employee of his cousin. Maybe he thought that the uncle should have left a share in the ranch to him. This sense of injustice could have been what was gnawing at him and making him so morose.

Or it might have been an ulcer. Or being married to Molly.

★   ★   ★

He stayed about three weeks on the Circle T ranch, and thoroughly enjoyed it. Kitted out in high-heeled boots, Levis, check shirt and Stetson hat, he rode the range with Jed Johnson and had lessons in using a lasso without ever becoming adept at it. He noticed that some of the cowboys carried guns, but Johnson said they were more for ornament than use, though now and then there might be a rattlesnake to shoot. It appeared that the days of battles with rustlers and other badmen were long gone by, and quick-on-the-draw gunslingers were now strictly for the Hollywood movies.

He did, however, have quite an array of firearms in his gunroom, including an old Colt six-shooter with a long barrel which had been used in the early days, as well as a Winchester repeater and a buffalo rifle. But these were just collector's items, and his other rifles, shotguns and pistols were of a more modern design. He invited his guest to do some target-shooting with him; and Hector tried out the revolver he had bought in New York and never yet used. Johnson was pretty handy with all the guns, but Hector was not outclassed. He had long been proficient with the Lee Enfield rifle, which he had carried in the Great War, and had learned to use a revolver in the Black-and-Tans.

'Where'd you get yourself the gun?' Johnson asked.

Hector told him about the raid on the jeweller's shop in New York and the shooting. 'I thought that in such a violent country I might need some personal armament.'

Johnson laughed. 'And how many times have you had to protect yourself from attack?'

'Not once. Maybe I'm just lucky.'

He had once been threatened with a gun; but that had been by a woman, and her object had been a benign one. He felt no inclination to tell Johnson about this incident; it was hardly to his credit.

'Could be you are at that,' Johnson said.

* * *

It really was the good life; horse-riding, helping to round up cattle, being waited on in the big house by black servants. But it could not go on for ever; it would have to end sometime, because he would never have been content to take a job as one of the hired hands even if Johnson had offered to employ him. It would have been too much of a comedown after living in the big house like an honoured guest. And besides, he had begun to tire of it; the novelty wore off and he knew it was time once again for a change.

That it came sooner rather than later, however, was because of the women. Almost from the start he could detect signs that they were both attracted to him, and he was careful to avoid giving any indication that he was willing to play that kind of game. It would have been crazy with both husbands in close attendance. And for the first couple of weeks or so he managed to steer clear of trouble. Then one day Paula suggested that he might accompany her into town, where she had some shopping to do.

'You could drive me there in the Chrysler.'

Hector told her he was afraid he could not do that because all he had driven so far was a Model T Ford, and that was rather a different kind of animal.

'No matter,' she said. 'I'll teach you.' She glanced at Johnson who was present at the time. 'Don't you think that would be a good idea, Jed? Hector really ought to learn to drive a decent automobile.'

Hector could tell that Johnson was not much in favour of the suggestion; but to raise any objection would have been as much as to say that he did not trust his wife to go into town with the guest whom he himself had invited into the house. So he said:

'Well, if it's okay with you, Hec.'

And what could Hector say but: 'Why, certainly. I'll carry your parcels if you want me to, Paula.'

'So that's settled,' she said; and she went away to get herself ready for the trip.

19

Driving Lessons

Molly had not been present when the arrangement was being made, but Hector caught sight of her coming out on to the portico as they drove away. She waved an arm, and he thought she might have been shouting something, but he could not hear what it was. Possibly she was trying to stop them, so that she could join the party. Whether Paula noticed her or not, he could not be sure; but if so she ignored the other woman and drove straight on without looking back.

Soon after they had got on the hard road she stopped the car and changed places with Hector. She gave him instructions regarding the use of the pedals and the gear lever and told him to go ahead. He was a quick learner and soon got the hang of things, his experience with Snitzler's van standing him in good stead. There was not much traffic on the road, and she let him take the car into town, which was a place called Simsville. It was of no great size, and practically all the commercial activity seemed to be confined to Main Street, a wide thoroughfare running almost dead straight through it. It was what Americans themselves would have called a hick town, and Hector could imagine it in the old wild days being the scene of much drunken roistering and not a little gunplay. It was quieter now, and there were no gunfighters stalking the streets or pushing their way through the batwings into the saloons; though there were still some horses around and a number of carts and buggies.

He trailed round with Paula as she did her shopping, acting as porter; and then they had coffee in a snack bar and talked a bit of this and that before returning to the car. On the way back to the ranch she gave him some more driving instruction, and he got the impression that during the whole of the outing she was putting herself out to be particularly charming to him. Now and then her hand would touch his, which might have been merely for the purpose of the lesson, but which he sensed could well have been rather more than that. He was wary; he wanted to avoid any kind of involvement with Jed's wife, because that could only lead to trouble; but he could read the signals she was putting out, and there were unmistakable indications that she was fully prepared to act recklessly even if he was not.

'You know, Hector,' she said, 'you've really livened things up for us since you came to the ranch. Life can be so boring when you have the same old faces round you day after day, the same dull routine. Sometimes I just feel like screaming my head off.'

'I'm surprised to hear that,' he said. 'I'd have thought that with so much to do, boredom would be the last thing you'd suffer from.'

'Well, you're wrong. I feel trapped; I feel like I'm in a cage and never going to escape. And then somebody like you comes along; somebody who's free to come and go as he pleases; and I see what I'm missing.'

'It may not be much at that. I wouldn't rate my way of life very highly in the enjoyment stakes. It's hand-to-mouth, just hand-to-mouth, I can tell you.'

'All the same,' she said, 'I guess I'd take it if I had the chance.'

And when she said this she put a hand on his knee and looked at him in a way that told him without doubt what she had in mind. And it was so crazy it simply did not bear thinking about. Unless she had money of her own. And even then it would have been no better than that other business had been with Clara Millbank; which now seemed so long

180

ago it might almost have been in another life.

They had stopped to change places at the wheel again when this conversation took place, and she seemed in no hurry to get the Chrysler going again. She was leaning towards him, and he had a feeling that at any moment she might put her arms round his neck and pull him towards her for a kiss. And he would not have minded it; he would not have minded it at all if the circumstances had been different; for she really was one hell of an attractive woman. But he had to think what it might lead to; and the name of that was trouble.

So he made no move on his part; and after a moment or two she gave a laugh, as if to tell him it was all a bit of playful nonsense and not to be taken seriously. And then she put the car into gear and got it moving on the homeward track.

★   ★   ★

Molly was in a bad mood; it was apparent in her expression when they went into the house. She looked sulky and was pouting.

'You didn't tell me you were going into town.'

'Oh,' Paula said innocently, 'did you want to come along?'

'Of course I did. Didn't you see me waving to you to stop?'

'No, I didn't. Sorry, dear.'

She did not look sorry. It was obvious to Hector that she had never had any intention of taking Molly along with them, and had purposely avoided telling her about the proposed outing. Molly probably guessed that too, and it was making her mad. Hector felt like piggy-in-the-middle, and he did not care for that position.

★　★　★

Next day Paula suggested that, as she had nothing better to do, she might as well take him for further driving lessons in the Chrysler.

'I suppose we can have it, Jed?'

Johnson looked as if he would have liked to say no, but could think of no good reason for refusing.

'I guess so, but maybe Hector would rather go riding on horse-flesh than on the seat of an automobile.'

So there was the opening left for him to take if he wished to. And he thought about it; but it would have been too much of a slap in the face for Paula, and he was pretty damned sure she would not take at all

182

kindly to the rebuff.

'Well,' he said, 'maybe I do need another lesson or two. I'm not so hot on the gear changes.'

That was when Molly walked into the room and wanted to know what was going on. Johnson told her at once. Hector thought he seemed eager to do so; perhaps anticipating that she would want to go along too.

'Paula's taking Hector in the Chrysler for more driving lessons.'

'Oh,' Molly said, 'is that so?'

'Yes, it is so,' Paula said. 'have you any objection?'

'Of course not. Why should I have? I think I'll come with you.'

'Oh no, dear. That wouldn't be at all a good idea. You'd only be bored.'

'I don't think I would. And I've nothing better to do.'

Paula frowned. 'But I can't give driving lessons with you sitting in the back and talking all the time.'

'I won't say a word. I'll be as quiet as a mouse.'

'You wouldn't be able to. I know you too well. You just have to chatter.'

'I do not so.'

They were both getting quite heated and beginning to snap at each other. Hector felt uncomfortable, and Johnson was just standing by, hands in pockets, saying nothing.

'Anyway,' Paula said, 'I refuse to give driving instruction with somebody in the back seat, and that's that.'

It finished the argument. Molly could bite her lip and look daggers at Paula as much as she liked, but there was no way she could insist on joining the party if she was not welcome. Jed too had to accept the situation.

★   ★   ★

They did not go to Simsville this time, but drove in the opposite direction, with Hector at the wheel. About five miles on there was a dirt road branching off to the left, and Paula told him to turn off there. The road went uphill, winding all the way, and after a while she told him to pull up at the side, which he did.

'Now,' she said, 'switch off the ignition and come with me. I'm going to show you the most marvellous view.'

There was a small wooded hill on the right, and she led the way up through the trees until they reached the summit.

'There,' she said. 'What do you think of that?'

It really was quite a sight. The rolling

grassland stretched away into the distance to where a small lake glinted in the sunlight; beyond it a line of hills rose along the horizon. Here and there were grazing cattle, miniaturized by distance, while off to the right the ranch house and the outbuildings and the corral with horses in it were just visible.

'It's fine,' he said. But he was sure she had not brought him there simply to admire the view.

And then she said: 'Why did you have to come here, Hector?'

'You asked me to.'

'Damn you!' she said. 'You know that's not what I meant. Why did you come to the ranch? You see what you've done, don't you? You've made two women fall in love with you. One would have been bad enough, but two — '

'No,' he said. 'I don't believe it. You're talking nonsense.'

'Am I? I don't think so.' She put a hand on his arm. 'You must have noticed.'

Which was true of course. But it was ridiculous nevertheless and could not be allowed to lead to anything, because that way disaster threatened. But it was obvious that she was not thinking along those lines; and suddenly she flung her arms round his neck and pulled his head down to hers with surprising strength and kissed him on the lips with a fierceness he would never have expected.

The sensible thing to do would have been to repulse her; to free himself from her embrace and tell her it was no go. But suppose she then became really mad at him? And suppose she had the Potiphar's wife syndrome and went to Jed with a story of how he had tried to seduce her, what then? The situation would be bad indeed. So when it came to the point he took the easy way, as he had done with Leila Wayburn, though there was no pistol to persuade him this time; only his own inclination. For the easy way was the enjoyable way, no doubt about that; because if there was one thing about Paula Johnson that was really undeniable, it was that she was one hell of a seductive woman.

★   ★   ★

'Driving lesson go well?' Johnson asked.

'Pretty well,' Hector said; and hoped there would be no more questions on that subject.

'He's a quick learner,' Paula said. 'Aren't you, Hector?'

And he could detect a glint of something in

186

her eye and a twitch of amusement on her lips.

'I do my best.'

It was evening, and they were sitting around having drinks. Johnson and Milligan were smoking cigars, but Hector had never taken to them and preferred a cigarette. The women were smoking cigarettes in long black holders. Molly was looking moody, possibly still brooding over that refusal of Paula's to let her join instructor and pupil at the driving lesson.

She said: 'Oh, I'm sure you do.' In a rather sarcastic way. 'And you have such a good teacher, don't you?'

Hector noticed that Johnson glanced at her sharply, but Milligan seemed uninterested; he just looked bored.

'Where did you go?' Johnson asked.

Paula told him.

'There's a fantastic view from up there,' Hector said.

'Yes, there is.'

'I wonder you had time to look at it,' Molly said.

Nobody made any comment on that, and conversation languished. It was then that Hector decided it might be best for all concerned if he brought his stay at the Circle T ranch to an end. He could see trouble looming like a dark cloud on the horizon if he stayed longer. And he was not sure he could handle it.

★ ★ ★

He awoke in the night to discover that someone had climbed into bed with him. The next discovery was that it was a woman and she was naked. It was dark in the room and he could not see who it was. But he could guess.

'Now this really is madness,' he said. 'You must know it is. If Jed — '

The woman gave a giggle, and he knew then that the guess had been way off the mark.

'Molly!'

'Yes, me,' she said. 'Aren't you pleased?'

'I'm petrified. Suppose Rory were to — '

'Oh, don't bother yourself about him. He sleeps like a log. And besides, I don't think he'd give a damn anyway.'

'All the same,' Hector said, 'I think you'd better go back where you came from. This is sheer lunacy.'

'Maybe it is. But it's nice, don't you think?'

She was snuggling up to him; and it was nice; he had to admit that, even if it was not at all wise.

'Now, Hector darling, you're not really going to throw me out, are you? That would be too too silly for words. I'm young, I'm here, I'm yours. What more could you ask for?'

What more indeed! And he could see that getting rid of her was going to be difficult; she was clinging to him like a limpet to a rock and obviously had no intention of letting him throw her out. To try it might have caused something of a racket; might have roused others. And he did not want that.

So yet again he took the easy way. And enjoyed it.

★   ★   ★

He broke the news at breakfast when they were all there.

'I shall be leaving today.'

They reacted in different ways. Johnson nodded approvingly; Rory Milligan showed no emotion whatever; Paula frowned but said nothing; and Molly, who had been looking very smug until then, as if calling to mind something that had pleased her very much, appeared simply devastated. She made no attempt to hide her dismay, but blurted out:

'Oh, but you can't! You can't!'

Johnson said: 'If the man wishes to leave

it's surely up to him to make the decision. We've been pleased to have you here, Hector, and you know you can stay as long as you like; but if you've made up your mind, that's it.'

'I have. I've greatly enjoyed being here, but it's getting on for a month, and I don't feel I can trespass on your hospitality any longer.'

'It wouldn't be a trespass,' Paula said. 'You should know that.'

'It's nice of you to say so, but I have to move on. I've a life to live.'

'Where do you aim to go?' Johnson asked.

'Back to England. America is fine, but I don't think I'm going to strike it rich here. Dollar bills don't grow on trees, as a man told me not long ago.'

'Maybe it's the right decision,' Johnson said. 'For you.'

'I think so.'

★ ★ ★

The rancher took him in the Chrysler to Simsville, where he was to catch a bus to carry him on the first leg of his journey home. Before they parted Johnson handed him a sealed envelope.

'Something to help you on your way.'

'I don't know that I can take this,' Hector

said. He guessed there was money in the packet.

'Sure you can,' Johnson said. 'From one buddie to another buddie. Hell, I got plenty.'

'Well, thanks, Jed. Thanks a lot.'

They shook hands and parted.

★   ★   ★

He opened the envelope on the bus. There were ten one-hundred-dollar bills in it. It was generous of the man; but perhaps he felt that getting rid of the cuckoo in the nest was cheap at the price, even though the cuckoo would have gone anyway.

For Hector the money was more than welcome; without it he would not have known how to obtain the steamship ticket back to England. Not being a seaman, he doubted whether he could have worked his passage.

★   ★   ★

He took the Colt revolver with him, and a few rounds of ammunition. He simply carried them through the Customs in his jacket pocket. It was dead easy.

20

Rock Solid

'So,' Arthur Langdon said, 'the land of opportunity didn't turn out to be all that you expected.'

Hector had a feeling that his father might have been quite disappointed if he had made good in America, because it would have proved him wrong in his prognostications. But perhaps that was rather too harsh a judgement on the old man.

His mother had been only too happy to welcome him back home, though she did berate him in a kindly way for neglecting to write more often during his absence. In fact he had sent no more than a couple of picture postcards during the whole of his stay in the United States.

'We were very worried about you, you know.'

'I'm sorry,' he said. 'There was so much to do. I was moving around quite a lot and didn't have much time for writing.'

'Well, you must tell us all about it sometime. I'm sure it's a very interesting story.'

He promised to do that, but wondered just how much to tell. The story would have to be very carefully edited.

His father was of course yet again anxious to know what he intended doing now that he was back in England.

'Have you anything in mind?'

He had to admit that he had not.

'But I'll take a look round. I'm sure I'll soon find something.'

Rather to his own surprise, he did, though it was not the kind of job that was calculated to meet with Arthur Langdon's whole-hearted approval. A local bus company was advertising for drivers as it expanded its services in the county, and on a whim he applied. He thought it might be fun.

He was taken on, put through a brief training course, and within a few weeks found himself driving a yellow bus between Norwich and a village twenty miles to the south called Maythorpe. The route passed through a number of other villages of varying sizes, and the road was winding, very narrow in parts, and untarred. In dry weather the bus raised clouds of dust; when it was wet there were puddles and mud. He loved it, and took no notice of his father's stated opinion that it was not the kind of occupation he would have expected a son of his to be engaged in.

'Might as well be an engine-driver.'

Hector was not in the least bothered by this criticism, and he had soon moved out of his parents' house and was living in lodgings in Maythorpe. This was a sensible move, since the final run of the day terminated at the village, where the bus was accommodated overnight in a large shed at the rear of a one-time coaching inn called The Fox and Hounds. Hector had a room at the inn, which was very convenient. His conductor, a man named Henry Reeder, lived in the village too, but he lodged with a postman and his wife. Reeder was a podgy, cheerful young man, and he and Hector got on well together.

It was very soon after his move to Maythorpe that Hector met Eva Gray. It was at a dance in the village hall, an old army hut with a stage at one end, where a five-piece band was doing its stuff with a preponderance of saxophone and drum. She was with a party of friends, and he just went up to her and said:

'Hello! I'm Hector Langdon. Will you dance with me?'

She looked at him, and in a way it was like that first meeting in Dublin with Noreen O'Hare. There was the same kind of spark or whatever it was passing between them, the same instant recognition of mutual attraction.

Only this time he knew it was for keeps. He just knew.

Maybe she knew it too. For she did not hesitate; there was no wavering; just the one word: 'Yes.'

Three months later they were married.

★　★　★

At the time of their meeting she was living with her brother, Edward Gray, his wife Mary and their son Martin. She was working as a clerk in the office of an estate agent in the village.

Gray was a corn merchant and miller. He had a windmill half a mile out of the village and some twenty acres of land. He employed half a dozen men, reared pigs as a sideline, and was reputed to be pretty well off. The mill house was not particularly large, but it was well built and in good condition. There was a pump in the kitchen for water, oil-lamps for lighting and a coal-fired range for cooking.

The Grays were not entirely in favour of Eva's engagement to Hector Langdon. They had known him for so little time, and a bus-driver could hardly be rated as the best of matches. But of course it had also to be remembered that his father was a respected

Norwich solicitor, and that was certainly in his favour. Besides which, it could not be denied that he was a most charming young man; no one could help liking him. The question still remained: was he quite the right husband for Eva, who was, it had to be admitted, rather a giddy creature? There could be no doubt that the couple were very much in love; but would it last? That was the question.

It was a question that Arthur and Frances Langdon also asked themselves; and they too could not be sure of the answer. They feared it was not the most promising of marriages; they knew Hector's character too well. And Eva Gray, though a pretty and delightful little thing, did not strike them as being the sort of person to keep their son from going off the rails. However, they could do nothing about it and could only hope for the best.

At least the newlyweds would have no trouble in finding a home. There was a cottage that Edward Gray owned; it adjoined his property and was standing empty. All it needed was a lick of paint and some repairs here and there, which he immediately put in hand; and then it would be quite perfect for the happy pair if they wanted it.

They did. And as soon as the honeymoon, which was spent at Brighton, was over, they moved in. The elder Langdons had paid for most of the furnishing, and it was as cosy as anyone could have desired.

There was only one fly in the ointment: Hector was no longer employed by the bus company. He had been far too erratic in his behaviour. Often he would be late in setting out with the bus, which meant that would-be passengers were left waiting on the roadside, kicking their heels and wondering when the transport would turn up. Then he would drive at a hectic speed to make up for lost time, swinging round bends much too fast for the comfort of the passengers and recklessly overtaking carts and cyclists. At other times he would find himself ahead of schedule and would stop the bus at the side of the road while he smoked a cigarette and chatted with Henry Reeder. It was all a game to him, but it was a game that had to come to an end. There were too many complaints about his conduct coming into head office, and he was given the push.

It was not the most auspicious of starts to married life, but it bothered him very little, and Eva was not worried either. She had kept her job with the estate agent, and surely something would turn up for Hector before very long.

'I believe in you, darling. I always will.'

'I'd be very disappointed if you didn't,' he said. 'But it's nice to hear you say it.'

'I love you so much. So very much.'

'And I love you more than anything else in the world.'

'How awful it would have been if we'd never met.'

'Doesn't bear thinking about, does it?'

'It must have been fated.'

'In the stars,' he said. 'Most certainly in the stars.'

It was yet early in their married life. There was no thought in either mind that anything could possibly go wrong. Other marriages faltered of course, hit the buffers, went down the drain. But this was different; this was special; this was theirs — rock solid.

★ ★ ★

In the event he did not have to wait long before getting another job. And in this his brother-in-law, Edward Gray, was able to help him. Gray had dealings with a large flour-milling company in Norwich, and their representative made periodical calls on him for orders of by-products such as middlings and bran, which were used in pig and poultry feed. This man, Thompson, was just coming up to his retirement and the firm was looking for a replacement, as he informed Mr Gray.

'Have they anyone in mind?' Gray asked.

'Not as far as I know,' Thompson said.

It seemed too good an opportunity to let slip. Gray asked Hector whether he would be interested, and he said he would. So Edward Gray got in touch with the millers, put in a word of recommendation, and the upshot was that Hector went up to Norwich, met the bossman and got the job. It was sheer personality that did it. He knew nothing about the milling trade, but he was supremely confident that he could handle it. And as things turned out, he was right.

The fact was that people liked him; he had that certain way with him. Sales talk was hardly necessary; he would gas away about anything under the sun that was completely unconnected with the business in hand, and then, just as he was leaving, the customer would give him the order. It was as simple as that. For him.

★ ★ ★

'So,' Arthur Langdon said, 'my son is now a commercial traveller, a common bagman.' He sniffed. 'Well, I suppose it's a shade better than a bus-driver.'

'The pay is certainly better,' Hector said.

It was just as well, because soon there was a baby on the way and Eva would have to leave her job to look after it.

His mother was delighted at the news of an addition to the family. 'Now he really will have to settle down,' she said to Arthur. 'He'll be a father and we shall be grandparents. Isn't it wonderful?'

She had already lent him the money to buy a car. It was a bullnose Morris Cowley two-seater with a dickey-seat at the back. The milling firm supplied no car. Old Thompson had done his travelling by bus and train; he probably could not have driven a car anyway. Hector used the Morris and charged the firm travelling expenses. He covered a wide area and often had to sleep away from home. That was the only snag; he would rather have been with Eva, and she would rather have had him there.

But they were both happy. Nothing had yet come up to cloud their marriage. They both believed it would go on like that for ever.

21

Souvenir

Martin Gray was just six years old when Crystal was born. He was not overjoyed at the event; babies were not really in his line. But he idolized both of the parents. For the first few years of his life Aunt Eva had been living in the same house, and he loved her almost as much as he loved his mother. She was so lovely, and of course she was much younger than Mary Gray and always seemed to have time to play with him.

He did not miss her so much when she moved out because she was still quite close at hand; and now there was Uncle Hector too, who had soon become a hero to him. He had done so much: he had fought against the Germans in the Great War; and then he had gone to Ireland for more fighting; and perhaps best of all, he had been to America and had ridden with Texas cowboys.

Martin's father had of course fought in the war also; but he had been in Palestine and had not been up against the Germans but the Turks. When very young he had confused these latter in his mind with turkeys, and it seemed strange to him that anyone should have to fight what had always appeared to be quite harmless creatures, even if they did make a curious gobbling sound.

Uncle Hector was so different from his father in every way. He even looked like a hero; and he would tell wonderful stories about cowboys and Indians and gunfights with cattle rustlers, in all of which he had apparently taken part.

Once, when he was older, Uncle Hector showed him his revolver and explained how it was loaded and how you aimed and fired it, though he never went so far as to shoot at anything. Martin was fascinated by the weapon, and would have loved to have it when he played with his pals from the village; it would have given him so much prestige. But, of course, although Uncle Hector allowed him to handle it without any bullets in the cylinder, he would certainly never have allowed him to keep it even for a day.

His mother was not at all pleased when he told her about the gun. She already knew that Hector owned it, but she thought it was wrong of him to show it to her son. Sometimes Martin had a feeling that she did not altogether approve of Uncle Hector; though he could not see why.

He was about ten years old when the revolver
came into Mill House. Hector asked Edward
Gray to keep it for him, because Eva did not
like to have it in the cottage.

'She's got this stupid idea into her head
that someone might get killed.'

'Whatever makes her think that?' Gray asked.

'God knows. You know her. It's a sort of
obsession.'

'But you've had it there ever since you
came to live in the cottage. What's suddenly
brought this on?'

'With her there doesn't have to be a reason.
It's just one thing after another. Anyway, she
says if I don't get rid of it she'll throw it away
sometime when I'm not there.'

'Do you think she would?'

'I wouldn't put it past her. And I'd be sorry
to lose the gun. It's a kind of souvenir.
Reminds me of things. So will you hang on to
it for me? Just for the present.'

With some reluctance Edward Gray
agreed.

★ ★ ★

Mary Gray was not at all happy about it. The
idea of having a lethal weapon in the house

203

was not one that appealed to her in the least. But Edward had already taken it from Hector and was disinclined to hand it back to him.

'It'll be quite safe here.'

'And why wouldn't it have been safe where it was?'

'Hector says Eva is afraid somebody might get killed.'

'Well,' Mrs Gray said, 'it's easy to guess who she thinks that somebody might be.'

'He wouldn't!' Edward Gray sounded quite shocked. 'It hasn't gone as far as that, surely.'

'Perhaps not. But he's got quite a temper, you know. And she's playing with fire.'

★　★　★

Though he was not supposed to, Martin overheard this conversation, and he remembered something that Crystal had told him. It was that her father and mother sometimes had the most awful rows, and would even start shouting at each other and throwing things. She was not sure what it was all about, but it frightened her. She would go and hide in a cupboard until they calmed down.

It saddened Martin to hear such things about two people he had so much regard for. He had always thought them both perfect, and hated to think that they were not.

But the presence of the revolver in Mill House excited him. And he soon discovered where it was kept. There was a bureau in the living-room, and in the bureau was a secret cubby-hole. Unknown to his father or mother, he had long since discovered how to gain access to this by pressing a small projection. He guessed that this was where the gun would be put, and at the first opportunity when he was alone in the house he proved that his guess was correct: the revolver was there with half a dozen bullets.

★ ★ ★

It was at about this time that the sails were taken off the windmill because they had become unsafe, and the tower was capped with galvanised iron sheeting. Taking its place in a long shed built for the purpose was an oil-engine, and the millstones were taken out of the old building and erected in the new one. So the mill-hand, a man named Ward, had also to become something of an engineer. The windmill had never been used to produce flour, but had ground chiefly barley and oats, and now and then rye and a little wheat, for local farmers, the meal being used as stock feed.

Martin was rather sorry that the sails had

gone, but the old mill was a fine place to play games in. There were three floors of diminishing diameter above ground level, and one could climb up to them by fixed ladders, which were beginning to get rather worm-eaten. Windows on each floor gave grand views, especially the top one.

One day he took Crystal to the top. She loved it. She was an adventurous little girl; but she told her mother and he was in hot water for putting his young cousin's life at risk. Suppose she had fallen! It hardly bore thinking about! Down all those steps!

He was forbidden ever to do any such thing again. He was also told not to play in the mill himself; an order which he ignored.

★ ★ ★

There was a tennis-court at Mill House. Mary Gray was a keen player, but Edward seldom played except when dragged in to make up a four for doubles. He was not much good at any outdoor sports. In contrast, Hector was the kind of man to whom all ball games seemed to come as second nature. Eva was erratic but with flashes of brilliance. Martin was always banished to the sidelines whenever adults were playing. Which was galling, because he was better at the game than some of them, young as he was.

As a concession, he was sometimes allowed on court when the light was getting too bad for any decent play and the dew was making the grass damp. Which was no good at all.

'You must wait until you're older,' his mother told him.

It seemed a long time to wait for a game of tennis.

★   ★   ★

One of those who often joined the tennis parties was a man named Stanley Cooper. He had recently taken over the small farm which was on the opposite side of the road from Edward Gray's property. In fact the farmhouse was not more than thirty yards from the cottage where Hector and Eva Langdon were living. You just crossed the road and there you were. It was an old clay-lump building with a thatched roof and a lean-to at one end. It was in a rather dilapidated state, but Cooper seemed either to lack the money to pay for repairs or simply could not be bothered.

He was quite a young man, and not bad-looking in a somewhat coarse sort of way. He was single and lived alone; the wife of one of the farm labourers coming in daily to do the chores and a bit of plain cooking.

He had made himself known to the Langdons soon after his arrival. He was that sort of man; gregarious and standing in no fear of being rebuffed.

Hector took a dislike to him at once.

'There's one with an eye to the main chance, if you ask me.'

'Aren't we all?' Eva said. 'Don't be so uncharitable. He's probably quite nice under that rough exterior.'

'I doubt it.'

Somehow Cooper wormed his way into the tennis group. Mary Gray could never remember actually inviting him. He just seemed to be there, and you could hardly tell him to go away. Besides which, he did a little business with Edward, which brought him to the mill anyway.

But like him or loathe him, no one could possibly have foreseen the disaster he was to bring upon them.

22

Tennis Party

Though perhaps they might have done, for the portents were there. And they were not entirely unobserved. It was only that no one could tell to what they might lead.

There was gossip. It was remarked that Eva Langdon paid rather a lot of visits to the house across the road when her husband was not at home and the daughter was at school. Cooper had two men working for him, and they did not go about with their eyes shut. They confided certain things to their wives, and the wives, as wives will, spread the word around.

Of course, people said, there might be nothing in it; just innocent neighbourly visiting by a young woman bored with her own company. But on the other hand . . .

Anyway, there were dangers in it. For rumours had a way of reaching every corner of a village, and eventually there would be some officious person who felt it his or her duty to inform Hector Langdon of what was going on, innocent or not. And then the fat would really be in the fire, because Hector was a man of spirit and even of temper. He was not one to turn a blind eye to what Cooper might or might not be up to in relation to his wife.

★   ★   ★

The explosion came one evening when there was a tennis party at Mill House. Cooper was there, and of course Eva, and two or three other people from the village. Martin, though he was in tennis shoes and had brought his racket, was as usual no more than a spectator and unofficial ball-boy during the early sets. He did not even have Crystal to talk to, because she was in Norwich, staying with her grandparents.

Hector was not present at the outset; he had not yet come home, so Eva said. He had probably got held up somewhere, but she had left a note for him and he would probably turn up later.

He did. But he had obviously not come with the intention of playing tennis, for he was still in his business suit and black leather shoes. Cooper and Eva were not playing at the time; they were sitting in the summer-house, which was near the court. They were not actually holding hands but they were close enough to be touching each other, and they were so earnestly engaged in conversation that they were quite unaware of Hector's arrival until he was standing in front of them.

The first thing he said was: 'Get away from my wife, you stinking bastard!'

It was spoken so loudly that everyone heard it, and it stopped the tennis straightaway. Nobody was going to continue smacking a ball around when there was such a compelling counter-attraction taking place nearby. Everyone was stunned, though all, so they said afterwards, had seen it coming for some time. What they could not understand was why it should have occurred just at that particular time and place.

They would have understood better if they had known that before returning home Hector had paid a visit to The Fox and Hounds for a drink, and while there he had got into a conversation with Henry Reeder, his former colleague on the buses. Reeder had already had a few drinks, and this had made him garrulous. Somehow Stanley Cooper's name came up, and Reeder gave a wink and said:

'If I was you I'd keep an eye on him.'

'Now what,' Hector said, 'do you mean by that?'

Reeder, suddenly aware that he had said

more than he intended, attempted to retreat. 'Oh, nothing, nothing.'

But Hector was having none of it. 'Damn that for a tale! You meant something.' He grabbed the lapel of Reeder's jacket and glared at him. 'Out with it, man, out with it. Why should I keep an eye on Cooper?'

Driven into a corner, Reeder could see no way out but by repeating the gossip that was being passed around and of which Hector was probably the only one in Maythorpe who had not heard. Even Edward Gray had got wind of it, and had discussed with his wife the question of whether or not they ought to tackle Eva on the subject. In the end they had done nothing, though it had certainly worried them.

Reeder was alarmed by the effect his revelation had on Hector. Not that there was any great outburst of rage; quite the contrary in fact. He became suddenly very calm and released his grip on Reeder's lapel.

'Thank you, Henry,' he said. 'Thank you for telling me this.'

It was this icy calmness that struck Reeder; that and the look in Hector's eyes.

'There may be nothing in it,' he said. 'You know how people talk.'

'Yes, I do know how people talk,' Hector said. 'They just haven't talked to me. That's the trouble. Maybe they should have.'

He went away then without finishing his drink.

'Another man,' Reeder said when telling the tale, 'might have had a lot more drinks, winding himself up. But not him; he just walked out. But I could see how angry he was. I wouldn't have wanted to be in Cooper's shoes.'

So Hector had driven home, found the note and gone straight on to the tennis party, confident that he would find Cooper there.

★   ★   ★

Cooper said: 'I don't think you should have called me that, old boy. What's up with you? Have you been drinking?'

'Stand up,' Hector said.

Cooper did not move. 'Why should I? I'm quite comfortable where I am.'

Hector seized him by the left arm and hauled him to his feet. Cooper tried to break free but could not. Hector dragged him out of the summerhouse and knocked him down with a fist to the jaw. No one ran to help him up, and for the present he stayed where he had fallen, rubbing his jaw and staring malevolently up at his assailant, but showing no sign of any eagerness to engage in a fight with him.

But Eva had sprung up from her seat and had grabbed her racket.

'You beast!' she said; and struck Hector on the shoulder.

He hardly seemed to feel it. He turned and took the racket from her, let it fall to the ground and stamped on it. Then he picked it up and threw it away. It sailed high over the stop-netting at one end of the court and landed in a flower-bed twenty or thirty yards distant.

He spoke to Cooper, who was still sitting on the ground and massaging his jaw where Hector's fist had struck it.

'Stay away from her, do you hear? Stay away from her.'

Cooper managed to conjure up a sneer. 'And if I don't?'

'I'll kill you.'

These last words were spoken quite softly, but everybody heard them. They were so incisive, and no one else was saying anything; they were all enthralled by the unexpected drama.

Hector turned to Eva. 'Now you're coming home with me.'

She stamped her foot in anger. 'I am not.'

He did not argue with her; he simply grasped her arm and forced her to go with him. And again nobody interfered.

It was the end of the tennis for that evening. Nobody could take any interest in further play, and the visitors were not slow in taking their leave. They could hardly wait to spread the story of what had happened at the Mill House tennis party.

Martin had witnessed it all, and he was delighted to see Uncle Hector knock Mr Cooper down. He had never liked the man, who had a way of addressing him as Sonny Boy, which he resented. He was sorry to think that Aunt Eva, whom he loved so much, should have had anything to do with him. She should have been able to see what a rotter he was. It thrilled him to hear Uncle Hector say he would kill Cooper. He wondered whether he would. But perhaps there would be no need. Perhaps the threat would be enough to stop Cooper going anywhere near Aunt Eva in future. He hoped so.

★ ★ ★

For the next few days it was the talk of the village, and the general opinion was that Hector had done the right thing in knocking Cooper down. It was also anticipated that there would be no more fraternization between Mrs Langdon and the farmer across the way, now that Hector had put his foot down. On the other hand, Eva Langdon was a flighty young thing and headstrong; so there was no telling what might happen.

When nothing did happen, gossip and speculation died down. The matter appeared to be closed.

★   ★   ★

But not for long. Less than a week after the incident at the tennis party Stanley Cooper was found lying on his own back doorstep, as dead as could be. And the reason for his death was that he had been shot through the heart from very close range.

The bullet that had done the damage was later found imbedded in one of the inner walls of the kitchen. It was of .38 calibre and had almost certainly been fired from a pistol or revolver.

23

Interrogation

The snag was, from the point of view of the investigating police officers, that for the present no weapon of this description could be found.

The body had been discovered early in the morning by one of Cooper's farm labourers, a man named Walter Nodge, who had just arrived for work. He said that at first he had thought his employer was dead drunk, as he had been on sundry other occasions, but closer examination revealed the fact that he was not drunk but was most certainly dead.

'Give me quite a turn, it did,' Nodge said.

Having recovered from the turn, he decided to ride his bike down to the village police station and inform the sergeant of what he had discovered. It was the sensible thing to do, and it set the wheels of the law in motion.

A detective inspector named William Wright of the county police was leading the investigation, and it was not long before he gleaned the information that the dead man had recently been threatened by his close neighbour, Mr Hector Langdon. Even the precise words of the threat, 'I'll kill you,' were repeated by more than one witness.

Not surprisingly, therefore, Hector, returning from work late in the afternoon, found himself apprehended by the police and subjected to some sharp interrogation.

In answer to the question of whether or not he had in fact used the words, 'I'll kill you,' when addressing Mr Stanley Cooper on the occasion of a tennis party at Mill House on a certain date he freely admitted that he had.

'But it was not meant to be taken literally. We all say things like that in the heat of the moment, don't we?'

Detective Inspector Wright did not say whether we all did it or not. He said: 'And in the heat of the moment why did you think it necessary to threaten him, sir?'

Somewhat reluctantly Hector answered: 'I was warning him to stay away from my wife.'

'Why?'

'Because,' Hector said; and hesitated, not wishing to admit that he had any doubts concerning his wife's behaviour. 'Because I'd heard rumours.'

'Rumours that she'd been having an affair with Mr Cooper?'

'Something of that sort, yes.'

The interrogation was taking place in a

room at the Maythorpe police station. Hector was not under arrest — yet. He was simply helping the police with their inquiries. A detective constable taking notes was also present. The room was chilly; it was plainly furnished with a high wooden desk, a tall stool to go with it, a battered deal table, a hard bench and three hard chairs. It reminded Hector of a railway waiting-room; it had the same rather unpleasant odour and the same lack of comfort.

Detective Inspector Wright sucked his teeth and said: 'Do you, Mr Langdon, possess a pistol or revolver?'

Hector hesitated again for a moment before answering: 'No.'

The momentary hesitation did not go unnoticed by the inspector. He was a large, florid, ponderous man in an ill-fitting suit. From his appearance he might have been judged to be slow-witted. The judgement would have been wrong.

'Now let's get this straight,' he said. 'You arrived home from work yesterday at nine p.m. Is that correct?'

'About that time, yes.'

'You'd had a long day, hadn't you?'

'It happens occasionally. I have a large area to cover.'

'Yes, of course. And when you arrived

home did you notice whether any light was showing in Mr Cooper's house?'

'Yes, there was.'

'But you saw no signs of activity?'

'No.'

Wright had already confirmed from Walter Nodge that when he found the body two oil-lamps were still burning in the house, and it was evident that the killing must have taken place after dark the previous day. The police surgeon had confirmed this, although he could give no exact time when the death had occurred.

'Mrs Langdon was not in your house when you returned, you say?'

'No. She came in about half an hour later. She'd been spending the evening with friends in the village.'

'And neither of you heard a shot being fired, then or later?'

'No. We should almost certainly have heard it if there had been one while we were there. But there was nothing.'

The interrogation went on for a while longer; but eventually Hector was allowed to go, with the warning that he would probably be needed for further questioning and should keep himself available.

★ ★ ★

Edward Gray was in something of a quandary. He and Mary had been away from Mill House at the time when the shooting might well have taken place. They had gone to Norwich in the Rover in the afternoon; had done some shopping and had gone to the Haymarket Cinema in the evening. They had not returned until about a quarter past ten, and so had heard nothing of the shooting. It was doubtful whether they would have heard a pistol shot anyway, seeing how far Mill House was from Cooper's place. Martin had been in the house, but he said he had heard nothing.

The quandary that Edward Gray was in while the police were questioning him had to do with the revolver he was keeping in the bureau for his brother-in-law. He wondered whether he ought to mention it, but finally decided not to. And Mary said nothing about it either.

But as soon as the police had gone he went to the bureau to see if the weapon was still there, and to his consternation discovered that it was not. It was obvious that Hector must have been to the house during his and Mary's absence and taken it. But when? Well, the answer to that was that he could have done it at almost any time in the past few days. He came and went much as he pleased

221

and could have chosen a moment when there was nobody in the living-room. He knew where the gun was kept and how to open the cubby-hole. It would have taken him hardly a minute to stow it in his pocket and walk out again.

Edward and Mary conferred together on the subject, and they had to face the fact that things looked bad for Hector.

'Oh, my God!' Mary said. 'Do you think he can have done it?'

In his heart Edward thought it was only too likely; but he did not say so. He had to try not to believe the worst, though it was difficult not to. The very fact that Hector should have taken the gun in that furtive way was in itself highly suspicious.

'It's Eva's fault,' Mary said. 'What could she have seen in that man?'

Edward sighed. He loved his sister, but he could not help feeling that she was indeed much to blame. It was a bad business all round.

★   ★   ★

It was two days after the shooting when the police search for the murder weapon was finally successful. It was found in a cesspool at the back of the pigsties in Cooper's

222

farmyard. They were dragging the pool with a garden rake when out of the thick, stinking sludge a revolver appeared. When it had been cleaned it was found to be a Colt .38 calibre weapon. There were two live cartridges still in the cylinder and one empty case. The only possible conclusion was that the bullet that had killed Stanley Cooper and had later been found in the kitchen wall had come from this empty case.

The question that now remained to be answered was: to whom did the revolver belong?

★   ★   ★

Edward Gray heard about the discovery of the gun, and having conferred again with his wife, decided he could no longer conceal from the police the facts about the weapon.

'It's gone too far now. I have to consider my own position. I could be in very deep trouble for withholding information. It's a criminal offence.'

'I suppose you're right,' Mary said. 'Indeed, I'm sure you are. It's certain now that Hector did the killing, and he'll have to face the consequences. He can't expect you to shield him.'

Detective Inspector Wright looked grim

when Edward Gray told him that he had been holding the revolver in his bureau for Hector Langdon.

'Why?' Wright asked.

'Because his wife didn't like having it in their house.'

He did not add that she thought somebody might get killed. He thought it better not to mention this.

'And why,' Wright said, 'didn't you tell us about this before? You must have known we were searching for the murder weapon.'

'Yes, I did. But I thought the revolver was still in my bureau, so it couldn't have been that.'

'It didn't occur to you, of course, to take a look in the bureau to make sure, Mr Gray?' Wright spoke with a touch of sarcasm.

'No,' Edward Gray said, 'it didn't.' And he knew that the inspector did not believe him. In Wright's shoes he would not have believed it either.

The interview was taking place at the Maythorpe police station, which had come to be the centre of operations for the murder investigation. It was not a building Gray had often visited, and he would have been happy not to have found it necessary to visit it now. In this instance he was not in the place for long. As soon as he had given his information to the inspector, action was quickly taken to arrest Hector Langdon and charge him with the murder of Stanley Cooper.

Unfortunately, from Wright's point of view, the man they wanted seemed to have disappeared.

24

Sentence

It seemed probable that, knowing the revolver would soon be found, and that when it was its ownership would quickly be discovered, he had decided that the game was up and his only possible course was to make a run for it.

He had told Eva that he would not be home for a night or two; but this was not at all unusual and she had thought nothing of it. There had in fact been very little conversation between them since the discovery of the murder. They both seemed wary of touching on that subject, as though it were something taboo. And in the prevailing climate nothing else seemed really worth talking about; all other matters faded into insignificance in comparison with that one forbidden topic. Both were glad that Crystal was away in Norwich with the old people. She would have asked so many questions which might have been difficult to answer.

The question always on the tip of Eva's tongue was: 'Did you kill him, Hector?'

And this was the one she dared not ask.

When the revolver was found she felt she knew beyond a shadow of doubt the only possible answer. But by then Hector had already departed.

★ ★ ★

A search for him was immediately begun when it was discovered by the police that he had not come home the previous night, and that Mrs Langdon could not tell them where he was. It was galling for Detective Inspector Wright to realize that he had allowed the chief suspect in the murder case to slip through his fingers, and he made every effort to make amends.

A clue to Hector Langdon's movements soon came to light in the shape of his Morris Cowley, which was parked in the yard outside Diss railway station. A booking clerk said that a man fitting Hector's description had bought a single ticket to London on the morning of the previous day. He had been carrying two suitcases.

The Metropolitan Police were alerted, and the hunt moved to the capital. It was of course possible that the fugitive had already made his way to Dover and thence to Calais. He had a passport and a head start on the pursuit.

Wright was furious. It would of course reflect on him. He would be blamed for carelessness. With hindsight he saw that he should have held Hector Langdon on suspicion while the search for the murder weapon went on; but he had not, and now the man had vanished.

But then, contrary to all expectation, Hector turned up again and presented himself at the Maythorpe police station. Questioned regarding the reason for his sudden departure to London, he replied that he had panicked and could think of nothing else but to get away. He had put up at a rather seedy hotel under an assumed name, and had hardly left his room during the time he was there.

'So why did you decide to come back and give yourself up?'

'I saw what a fool I'd been. I was simply drawing suspicion on myself. And I couldn't hide for ever. It had been sheer madness to cut and run. I knew I was innocent, but I had done the one thing which was certain to make people think I was not.'

'So,' Wright said, 'you still deny you shot Stanley Cooper?'

'Of course.'

'In spite of the fact that we have found the murder weapon, and it is a revolver which you gave your brother-in-law, Edward Gray, to keep for you?'

This seemed to floor Hector. He looked really taken aback.

'You found my revolver? Where?'

'As if you didn't know, Mr Langdon! Why, in the cesspool where you dumped it. It was very careless of you. Surely you must have realized we were bound to find it there eventually. But perhaps you figured it would give you a bit of time to get away.'

'No,' Hector said. 'You've got it wrong.'

But he spoke without conviction. All the wind seemed to have been taken out of his sails as a result of this damning evidence. Yet, as Wright had said, he must have known the gun would be found, unless he had somehow convinced himself that it would not. And perhaps, even if it was, he might have believed that Edward Gray would not reveal the fact that it was his and had been stored at Mill House. Were there any limits to the amount of self-deception a man in his position could indulge in? Could it even be that, feeling himself so fully justified in killing Stanley Cooper, he had convinced himself, not only that it was no crime at all, but that he had simply not committed it? Was he in fact mad?

Detective Inspector Wright had no such

far-fetched theory in his mind. What he saw before him was a man who, in a fit of jealous anger, had killed another man and was desperately denying having done so. But of course he would never get away with it. A judge and jury would see to that. If ever there was a man who was destined to end his days with a rope round his neck, it was this one.

★　★　★

The arrest of Hector Langdon on a charge of murder was quite naturally a subject of much debate in Maythorpe; and though most of the villagers had been in sympathy with him regarding the incident at the tennis party, it was pretty generally felt that shooting Cooper was going rather too far. You had to draw the line somewhere.

Eva was devastated. She had never believed that Hector would really carry out his threat to kill Cooper; it was just something people said, never having any intention of suiting the action to the words. But in Hector's case it had been different; he really had meant what he said, and had not been slow to carry out that final irrevocable act. And now it was as if her entire world had come tumbling about her ears.

She wept bitterly; but it was all too late for

that. The damage had been done and could never be repaired.

★   ★   ★

To Edward Gray it was a considerable annoyance; and that was putting it mildly. To have a brother-in-law arrested for murder was a terrible thing; it reflected so badly on him, innocent of any crime though he himself might be. When meeting people he felt awkward and self-conscious. Though no one mentioned the wretched business, he knew that it was uppermost in their minds. He could tell from the way they looked at him that they would dearly have loved to put all sorts of questions to him. He guessed too that they were all, if the truth were told, enjoying the whole affair, wallowing in the brief notoriety it had brought to the village.

'They love it, you know,' he told his wife. 'They can enjoy it because it doesn't touch them in any sensitive part. They're on the sidelines looking on. I hate to say it, but Hector really has let us in for a lot of trouble. And himself too, of course. What a fool! What a damned fool!'

'Yet it was Eva who started it,' Mary said. 'If she had behaved herself none of this would have happened.'

Edward glanced at her sharply. 'You don't suppose there was anything serious going on between her and that man?'

'I don't know. It's possible.'

'I never liked the fellow,' Edward Gray said. 'Thought too much of himself. And coarse with it. No manners. Pushed his way in where he wasn't welcome. Did we ever invite him here?'

'I don't know that we did. I fancy Eva brought him along.'

'There you are, then.'

He did not say where she was, but she knew what he meant, and she also knew how worried he was by the thought of what this affair might be doing to his reputation. But of course that was a minor concern compared with what poor Hector was facing. How awful it must be for him.

And also of course for Crystal. At the age of six she was old enough to appreciate what was going on, though she might not understand everything. She wondered how much the Langdons had told her. It was fortunate that she was with them, and for the present it had been thought best that she should stay there. Eventually of course she would have to come back and live with her mother, but just for now she was safely out of the way.

'When do you suppose the trial will take place?' she asked.

'I've no idea,' Edward said. 'I imagine it takes quite a bit of time for preparations to be made. Wretched business, hanging about. Much better to get it over and done with quickly. Better for all concerned.'

Except possibly for Hector, he thought. He was now languishing in Norwich jail; but uncomfortable as that might be, it was nevertheless life. He was still a young man and would not wish to die.

★   ★   ★

When the trial did take place it was regarded by everyone as little more than a formality. In Detective Inspector Wright's opinion it was an open-and-shut case. The evidence, though circumstantial, was surely so damning as to permit no doubt in the mind of even the most favourably disposed juror. In the Norwich courtroom where the proceedings took place learned counsel for the Crown and for the defence went over all the ground that had already been covered by the police inquiry, the one stressing all the unfavourable features of the evidence, and the other doing his utmost to make bricks with very little straw in order to build some kind of a rampart around his client.

Arthur Langdon, though taking no active part in the case himself, had engaged a fellow solicitor and a distinguished barrister to defend his son; but he knew in his heart that it was hopeless. He did not tell Frances so, and continued to make encouraging noises when talking to her about it. She, of course, was extremely distressed, but refused to believe that her darling Hector could possibly be guilty of murder. There had to be some terrible mistake. She prayed for him constantly, and trusted in God to save him from the gallows.

Arthur Langdon did not believe that God would do anything to prevent the law from taking its course and reaching the inevitable conclusion; but he would not for the world have said as much to her.

Edward Gray was a witness for the prosecution and had to give evidence, much against his will. He feared that he came out of the ordeal with very little credit. Eva also had to give evidence, and was very tearful while doing so. Mary Gray did not attend the trial; she gave as an excuse that someone had to stay at home and keep Martin company; the boy being very upset, as was to be expected.

Arthur Langdon was of course present every day, but not Frances, since Crystal was again staying with her grandparents and had to be looked after. In the child's presence Frances had to make an effort to appear cheerful even though her own spirits were low. Crystal might have been expected to ask a great number of questions, but she did not; she was unusually quiet. For the present she was being kept away from school, and she spent much of her time reading children's books and playing with her favourite toys.

⋆ ⋆ ⋆

There was only one surprise at the trial. It was that on the final day the prisoner suddenly altered his plea from one of 'Not Guilty' to 'Guilty'. He said he knew the case was lost, and he did not wish to go to his death with a lie on his lips. It was a question of conscience. He regretted what he had done, but the fact could not now be altered. He believed he had killed the man in a fit of madness while under great mental stress. It had been a crime of passion, but he knew that this was no excuse and he was prepared to take what punishment the law required.

He thanked his defence team for what they had done on his behalf, but perhaps after all it was better this way.

Mr Dakin, the solicitor and Mr Marley-Jones, the barrister, were confounded by this statement, made so calmly and so unexpectedly by their client, but they had to accept his decision.

After this the trial soon reached its climax. The judge put on the black cap and passed sentence of death.

Eva, sitting between her brother and her father-in-law, wept.

Hector looked at them and smiled briefly before being taken away.

25

Crazy

Crystal came back to live at the cottage with her mother soon after the execution. She was very quiet for a while; but it was remarkable how quickly she seemed to recover from an ordeal which for her had perhaps been as exacting as it had been for any of the others involved. She had adored her father, and his death had left a terrible gap in her young life. But it was this very youthfulness that came to her aid in this extremity. She did not forget, but life went on and she enjoyed it in spite of her bereavcment.

It was Eva who found the greatest difficulty in adjusting to the situation. She was plagued by a sense of guilt. For had it not been because of her that two men were dead, one by a bullet in the heart and the other by the hangman's rope? How could she ever rid herself of the bitter memory of that double tragedy and the part she had played in it? How was it possible that the dark shadow of those deaths should ever leave her?

Edward did his best to comfort her, telling

her that she should not blame herself, for she could not have foreseen what would happen. And even Mary Gray, who had never really liked her, did her best to rouse her from her despondency. But all to no avail.

'She ought to go right away from here,' Edward said. 'At least for a time. This place has too many associations; it won't let her forget.'

'But where would she go? And what about Crystal?'

'We could take her for a while, couldn't we?'

'I suppose we could. And it might be good for her. She's very fond of Martin. Hadn't you noticed?'

Edward Gray looked surprised. 'No, I hadn't, to tell the truth. What does Martin think about it?'

'I believe it rather amuses him. Being a kind of hero to her, you know. Of course she's too young to be a real playmate, but I think he tolerates her in a rather superior way.'

'Well,' Edward said, 'we shall have to see what can be done.'

But as things turned out there was nothing they could do except go with the tide of events. Fate was to be the deciding factor in their plans for the future.

And the instrument chosen by fate was

none other than the Morris Cowley two-seater that Hector had bought with money borrowed from his mother and never repaid.

Eva was using the car now. Hector had taught her to drive, but she had never been a good pupil. On one occasion she had hit a gatepost and damaged one of the front mudguards. And another time she had backed into a brick wall, having put the car into reverse gear rather than bottom. Too often she would allow her attention to wander when it should have been concentrated entirely on the driving.

So when she steered the bull-nose into a head-on collision with a heavy lorry it could have been pure accident. Or, on the other hand, bearing in mind her mental state at the time, the acute depression she was in, there had to be another possibility: that she had deliberately steered her car into the path of the approaching lorry in order to take her own life. The coroner gave her the benefit of the doubt and recorded a verdict of accidental death, but Edward and Mary Gray were not altogether convinced.

'Knowing how depressed she was.' Edward said, 'one really can't be certain it was an accident.'

Mary agreed. 'That's true. And I can't help feeling that she and Hector ought never to have married each other. The partnership was doomed from the start.'

'Oh, come! Isn't that rather a sweeping statement?'

'Perhaps. But true, I think. They were too much alike; both a little mad, you know.'

'And now that leaves Crystal.'

'Yes. Poor girl.'

★   ★   ★

With both parents now dead, there was of course no possibility of Crystal's remaining at the cottage. She was moved for a time to Mill House, and then more permanently to her grandparents' house in Norwich. They were very pleased to have her there, and soon got her a place at a very good school in the city. Formerly she had attended a private school in Maythorpe, run by two maiden ladies; the one where Martin had been taught before moving on to grammar school at the age of eight.

It seemed an excellent arrangement, acceptable to all concerned; and soon the young girl enjoyed almost complete domination over both doting grandparents, who saw in her the reincarnation of their only son in a somewhat different guise.

In the holidays she frequently stayed for

periods at Mill House and renewed the old relationship with Martin. He liked having her there, and could not help observing what an attractive girl she was becoming as she grew older. She had inherited her mother's rich golden hair, but it was straight rather than curly, and her features were not so doll-like. It was quite evident that she was going to be a real beauty.

In the summer they would often play tennis together on the Mill House court, where the fateful incident involving Hector Langdon and Stanley Cooper had taken place. At the age of eleven she was already a good player, and very athletic with her long slim legs and well formed body. But Martin was six years older, and she was no match for him. He usually let her win a few games and occasionally even a set, just to make her happy; but one day this generous action on his part brought about an unfortunate result.

'Don't do that,' she said.

'Do what?' he asked.

'You know jolly well what. You hit that one out on purpose. You keep giving me points; you know you do.'

He denied it, but she refused to accept the denial.

'Don't tell lies. I know what you think. Just because I'm a girl and younger than you, you

241

think you'll please me by letting me win a few games.'

'It's not true, Crys. You're pretty good; you really are.'

'I know I am. But I'm not as good as you, and you know it. But I don't want anything given to me. If I can't win on level terms I don't want to win at all. Right?'

'Right,' he said. 'If that's the way you want it.'

He finished off the set without allowing her to win another point.

'You beast!' she said. 'You rotten beast!'

She threw down her racket, burst into tears and left the court. He watched her in bewilderment. He had done what she demanded and this was the result. There was no understanding her.

But next day all seemed forgotten. They played together again and he gave her points without making the gift quite so obvious. And afterwards they sat in the summerhouse, drinking lemonade and resting after their exertions. And suddenly she said:

'You know I'm in love with you, don't you, Martin?'

He looked at her in surprise, thinking she was kidding, but she seemed perfectly serious. So he said: 'Now what kind of nonsense is this?'

'It's not nonsense,' she said. 'It's the truth. When I'm old enough I'm going to marry you.'

He laughed, making a joke of it. 'You've decided that, have you? Don't I have any say in the matter?'

'Of course you have. But you like me, don't you?'

'You know I do.'

'Well, then — '

'But liking is a long way off marriage.'

'You'll come round to it,' she said, 'when you get used to the idea. I can wait.'

★ ★ ★

When he was eighteen Martin got a job with a big insurance company in Norwich. He travelled up by train daily from Maythorpe Road railway station, which was a mile or so out of the village, cycling this distance each way in all weathers. Frequently he would spend the evening at the Langdons' house and catch a late train home. Thus he kept in touch with Crystal and occasionally took her out to the cinema or the theatre.

By the time she was sixteen she was becoming quite mature, and out of her school uniform and in a dress or jumper and skirt she looked so attractive that she caught the male eye and he felt proud to be seen out with her.

And she could be jealous too. Once when she happened to see him in the company of a girl from the office she was most put out and made quite a song and dance about it when she next met him.

'What's her name?' she demanded.

'Miriam.'

'That's a biblical name, isn't it?'

'I don't know. Is it important?'

'Is she religious?'

'I haven't asked.'

'Do you like her?'

'Not particularly.'

'Then why do you go out with her?'

It was a difficult question to answer. He had in fact been out with Miriam only the once. And the reason for that had been that she had made all the running. She had, as it were, thrown herself at him, and in the end he had made a date with her. But it had been a mistake. They had nothing whatever in common, nothing to talk about. He realized how empty-headed she was almost at once, but for the time he was stuck with her. However, he decided then and there that this would be the first and last time he took Miriam out on the town. One evening with her was more than enough.

Fortunately, Crystal did not press for an answer. She said: 'I thought she looked rather cheap and flashy. Not at all the type I'd have expected you to go for.'

'I didn't go for her. She went for me.'

'You could have brushed her off.'

'I will in future.'

'Promise?'

'Promise.'

After a while she said thoughtfully: 'You wouldn't call me cheap and flashy, would you?'

'Perish the thought.'

'But I go for you, don't I?'

'Yes, but that's different.'

'In what way?'

'Well, you're Crystal, aren't you? You're unique. There's no one quite like you.'

'And that's good?'

'It's very good.'

'Do you love me, Martin?'

'Of course I love you.'

'Oh, good!' she said. 'Now we're getting somewhere.'

'You're crazy,' he said. 'Just crazy.'

She smiled enchantingly. 'I know. It's the way I'm made.'

26

No Room at the Inn

In the summer of 1939 they were much together. They played tennis, went swimming, took bike rides into the countryside, saw all the latest films and the touring plays, went dancing. It was great just to be alive and young.

It was of course the lull before the storm, and dark clouds were gathering. Hitler was ranting at Nazi rallies and already chunks of Europe had been taken over by the German military machine. Belatedly, after Chamberlain's return from Munich in 1938 with his worthless scrap of paper, Britain was arming. The signs of imminent conflict were there for all to see.

Even these two young people, so intent on enjoying themselves, could not help but be aware of what was happening.

'There's going to be a war, isn't there?' Crystal said.

Martin admitted that it appeared inevitable. 'Hitler's got to be stopped before he grabs all Europe and more besides.'

'What will you do if it comes?'

'In that case I don't suppose I'll have any choice. I shall have to fight.'

She frowned. 'I don't want you to go.'

'I'm afraid your objections won't make much difference. My father and your father were in it last time, and it looks as if I shall be in it this time round. Our grandparents were luckier. All they had was the Boer War, and they left that to the professionals.'

'It's awful,' she said, 'just awful. Why do the politicians let us in for such things? What have we done to deserve it?'

To that he had no answer.

★ ★ ★

So the summer wore away and September came. And German armies moved into Poland and the die was cast. Britain and France were mobilizing, and Martin Gray decided not to wait to be called up but to volunteer for military service straightaway. But it was not until the end of October that he was eventually accepted and became a gunner in the Royal Artillery.

Crystal was secretly thrilled, though she was sad that he should be going away. She would miss him so much. But it was just what she would have expected her hero to do, and she was so proud of him.

Not that the hero had much in the way of heroics to perform for the first couple of years in khaki. The greater part of this time was spent on the south coast, watching the Channel and waiting for the Germans to come across after their conquest of France. It was dead boring: doing gun drill, cleaning the guns, going on courses, and wondering when the battery would be sent overseas. In the meantime he rose to the rank of lance-sergeant and benefitted from the increase of pay that his promotion brought him.

He was in constant touch with Crystal by correspondence, and he had a photograph of her, which he showed to his comrades just to make them envious.

Periodically he went home on leave and saw how rapidly she was growing up. And then, early in 1942, she joined the Women's Royal Naval Service and became a Wren. She was stationed at Portsmouth and not far from him; so that they were able to meet now and then. He thought she looked very smart in her uniform, and more lovely than ever.

In September they managed each to get a weekend pass, and arranged to go up to London and spend the time together. He was there first, and went to meet her at Waterloo

Station. As usual the place was chock-a-block with men and women in uniform, civilians appearing almost like intruders who had no business to be there. Martin was carrying his gas mask and a haversack with his small kit in it. The weather was mild, and he had left his greatcoat behind; he did not expect to need it.

When Crystal's train came in it released another flood of humanity from the tightly packed compartments and corridors. In this seething mass he did not spot her at first, and feared that some last-minute hitch might have prevented her from coming. His heart sank at the thought, but then he saw her approaching the barrier, and a moment or two later they were in each other's arms, embracing and kissing with that uninhibited abandon which seemed to have come with those perilous times.

'I didn't see you at first,' he said. 'I thought you might have missed the train.'

'And that would have bothered you?'

'I'd have been inconsolable.'

'What a nice thing to say.'

'You look gorgeous,' he said.

'Of course I do. I've had naval officers trying to seduce me.'

'And no wonder,' Martin said.

But he was none too happy to hear it. He

hoped she was joking, but he feared it might be true.

'Now,' she said, 'what do we do first?'

They had made no plans. It was getting on for noon, and they had the rest of the day and the whole of Sunday before they had to return to duty.

'Perhaps it would be as well to book a room somewhere.'

She smiled. 'Yes. Better not leave it until the last minute.'

'Let's be on our way then.'

In their innocence they had imagined it would be easy. A couple of hours later they had come to realize just how difficult it was to obtain accommodation anywhere in London at that time. All the hotels were booked solid. They did not give up easily, but in the end they had to accept the fact that there was no possibility of getting a room.

Just for a rest they went to a cinema in the West End, but had to stand in a queue for nearly an hour before getting in. When they came out there was an air-raid warning and they spent some time in a crowded shelter until the all-clear sounded. It was now dark and the blackout was in force. They were hungry, and Martin suggested they should go to a canteen on Liverpool Street Station, which he had used in the past and which stayed open all night. Crystal agreed, and they found a Tube station and got there by the subterranean way.

To gain access to the canteen it was necessary to push their way past a heavy canvas blackout curtain and climb a flight of stairs; and when they got to it they found it was crowded with service men and women. But most of these were birds of passage, and there was much coming and going, so that before long they were able to get seats at a table. There they devoured a meal of beans on toast and Lyons fruit pies, washed down with tea from an urn. And then they just sat there, smoking endless cigarettes and waiting for time to pass, since they had nowhere else to go. It was not what they had anticipated, but at least they were together, and that was something.

They were still there at two o'clock in the morning, yawning and sleepy. At that hour the number of customers had dwindled to a mere handful, and they were told that the canteen would be closing for an hour to allow the cleaners to do their work.

That hour they spent in the gloomy surroundings of the station. It had become chilly by then, and they would have been glad to have had the coats which they had deemed unnecessary. They found a seat and snuggled together for warmth and hoped there would not be another air-raid warning to send then to some crowded shelter.

'You know,' Martin said, 'I never expected the first night I spent with you would be in these surroundings.'

She laughed. 'I could think of nicer places.'

'I've made a complete hash of things, haven't I?'

'Don't blame yourself,' she said. 'How were you to know all the hotels would be full?'

'I should have guessed. The place is crawling with Yanks loaded with money.'

'Now don't be nasty about our American cousins. We need their help. We could never finish the job on our own.'

'Churchill said we could if we had the tools.'

'He was being optimistic. Or less than honest.'

In the grimy, smoky, echoing cave of the station nocturnal work was going on. Strings of trolleys piled high with mail-bags and hauled by little electric tugs came and went. Squaddies weighed down with kitbags wandered hopelessly here and there, searching for trains that were not where they should have been and possibly did not even exist. Other trains stood motionless at platforms waiting for engines to come and attach themselves to them, the carriages dark and featureless. It was like the setting of some gloomy French film, a scene from Zola's *La Bête Humaine*. It made the heart sink just to walk into that depressing place.

'I've been remembering something,' Martin said. 'Something you said a long time ago. I think you must have been eleven or twelve at the time.'

'I said a lot of things when I was that age. Lots and lots. Don't tell me you remember everything.'

'Of course not. But this was important. At least, I think so now. It sticks in my memory.'

'So tell me then. What did I say?'

'You said that when you were old enough you were going to marry me.'

'I said that?'

'You did.'

'And what did you say?'

'I can't remember. I don't suppose I took it seriously.'

'And now?'

'Now you are grown up.'

'Yes, I am, aren't I?'

'So how about it? Are you still of the same mind?'

'Yes,' she said, 'I'm still of the same mind. If you are. Are you?'

'You bet, I am.'

'But it's not on, is it? Not right now, I mean.'

'It could be. It just could be.'

'Ah!' she said. 'Now I see how it is. You have some plan in your head and you've just been waiting to tell me.'

'Maybe I have.'

'Well, out with it. Don't keep me on tenterhooks. What's the plan?'

'First, there's something I haven't told you before. There's a buzz going round that the battery will soon be going overseas, and the betting is on North Africa. Nothing official of course, but I don't think there's much doubt about it.'

'Oh dear!' she said. 'You're going to be in the thick of it.'

'It had to happen sooner or later. In a way, I'm glad.'

'Glad to be going away from me?'

'No, of course not. But it's what I joined to do, and it just doesn't seem right to me, this sitting around in England waiting for Jerry to come to me. He won't now; you can bet on that. With Russia in the game, he's got his hands full. So here's what I've been thinking. We're bound to get embarkation leave before we go, and you ought to be able to claim compassionate leave at the same time. So why don't we pick up a special licence and get married? Then we could go to some little hotel in the country for the honeymoon. How does that sound to you?'

She flung her arms round his neck in delight and smothered him with kisses.

'I take it,' he said, when he could get a word in again, 'that you're more or less in favour of the idea.'

'But of course, of course. I think it's marvellous. And all this time you've had this in your head and you've been keeping it back from me. Why?'

'Well,' he said, 'it's like this. I'd intended keeping it until we were somewhere a little more intimate, if you see what I mean.'

'Yes, I do see what you mean. And now of course we won't be.' She gave a laugh. 'Things don't always go quite according to plan, do they?'

Later, when they had discussed every aspect of the matter and weighed the pros and cons of a score of venues for the honeymoon, Crystal said: 'How do you feel about getting married to the daughter of a murderer?'

She sounded very serious, and perhaps a little worried. It was a subject that had never come up before, as though it were something that neither of them wanted to bring out into the open. But it had to be; it could not be suppressed for ever; and it seemed to her best that it should come out now, before they took this fateful step of uniting themselves, each to the other.

His reply surprised her. It was so completely unexpected.

'I feel nothing whatever about it. For the simple reason that I shall not be doing that.'

She looked and sounded puzzled. 'I don't understand. You're proposing to marry me, and I'm a convicted murderer's daughter. So — '

'You're not,' he said. 'You may think you are, but the truth of the matter is, you're not.'

She spoke impatiently: 'You're talking rot; you know you are. So why?'

He shook his head. 'I'm not talking rot. Not a bit of it. Uncle Hector didn't kill Stanley Cooper.'

'How can you say that? You know it's not true. He was tried and convicted. He even confessed to the killing.'

'I know. But he was lying when he confessed.'

'How do you know? How can you be so sure?'

'Because I know who really shot Cooper, and it wasn't your father.'

'Who, then? Who?'

He hesitated a moment, as though even

then feeling some reluctance to reveal the fact. But he knew that, having gone so far, he could no longer hold back the truth.

'I did,' he said.

'You!' she said. 'You!' And then in anger: 'Why are you saying this? Do you think it's joke? If so, you've got a warped sense of humour, and I don't think it's funny. You can see I'm not laughing.'

'Yes,' he said, 'I can see you're not. And it's no joke. It's the truth, the solemn truth. I shot Cooper, and Uncle Hector was hanged for a crime he never committed.'

She stared at him. 'You're serious, aren't you? You really are serious.'

'Never more so in my life.'

'But I don't understand.' She sounded bewildered and a little scared too. 'How could you have done it? You were too young. Only ten years old.'

'Eleven, coming up to twelve. Old enough to fire a revolver. Old enough to kill a man.'

'And you did? You really did?'

'Yes.'

'Oh, my God!' she said. 'Oh, my God!'

27

Only Yesterday

He remembered it so well, it might have been only yesterday. It had been twelve years ago, and it was there in his memory as firmly imbedded as a rock in a glacier. He would never forget, never, even if he came through this war and lived to a hundred.

It started, you might say, that evening in late August when Uncle Hector turned up at the tennis party at Mill House in a flaming rage. Aunt Eva and that swine Stanley Cooper were sitting in the summerhouse and talking to each other pretty intimately by all appearances. Uncle Hector just walked in and said: 'Get away from my wife, you stinking bastard!' He remembered the exact words.

Cooper said something then, and Uncle Hector told him to stand up. Cooper refused, and Uncle Hector hauled him to his feet and knocked him down with a blow to the jaw. It was splendid; it was just what he would have wanted his uncle to do.

But Aunt Eva had been furious; she actually hit Uncle Hector with her racket.

Hector took it from her, stamped on it and threw it away. It was picked up next day in one of the flower-beds, but it was never any more use; it had rained during the night, and the frame was warped and all the strings were ruined. It was a nearly new Slazenger racket too, and had cost quite a lot; so it was rather a shame really.

Then Uncle Hector took Aunt Eva's arm and marched her away, just like a policeman taking a criminal to the lock-up. After that the tennis party just broke up, so he never got the chance to have a game even in the bad light.

★   ★   ★

It must have been about four or five days later when his father and mother went off to Norwich in the car in the afternoon, and he was left at Mill House on his own. He mooched about for some time; had a look at Jacob Ward grinding barley; soon tired of that; went into the old windmill and climbed to the top floor to sample the panoramic view from the window after brushing away the cobwebs; came down again and went to look at the pigs in their sties; scratched their backs with a stick and listened to their contented grunting; felt bored and decided to pay a call on Aunt Eva.

As usual he went round to the back door, which was shut. It had a latch, and he lifted it and pushed the door open and walked into the kitchen. No one was in there, and he made his way to the little entrance hall and had a look into each of the two rooms opening off it. They were unoccupied, but when he had closed the second door he heard sounds coming from the floor above, and he guessed that Aunt Eva was doing some housework up there.

He did not call to her, but climbed the stairs which rose quite steeply from the hall. The stair-carpet deadened any sound of his ascent, and when he reached the landing he saw that the bedroom door on the right was slightly ajar. It was from this room that the sounds were coming, and they were much louder now. He was puzzled by them; there was some creaking and heavy breathing, as if Aunt Eva might be shifting a bit of furniture and making hard work of it.

He went to the door and peered into the room, and was shocked by what he saw. Aunt Eva was on the bed and Stanley Cooper was lying on top of her. They were both naked and it was what they were doing that was making the bed creak.

They had not seen him, and he did not stay. One glance was enough. Then he was retreating down the stairs and out of the cottage. He ran all the way home and shut himself in. He felt a mixture of emotions; grief and anger. He shed tears of both. The disenchantment was so great, it was hard to bear. His darling Aunt Eva and that horrible man! He would never have believed it possible if he had not seen it.

It was anger that gradually gained the upper hand. The tears dried and he began to think about what he ought to do. Should he tell Uncle Hector? He considered this for a long time, but finally ruled it out. What would Uncle Hector do? Attack Cooper? Knock him down again? Take a stick to him and give him a good beating? None of this would be enough. Cooper was such a brute, he did not deserve to live.

And it was then that the idea came to him. He would kill Cooper, and then Uncle Hector would never have to know anything about that scene in the bedroom. He and Aunt Eva would be reconciled, and all would be fine. It seemed so obvious a solution, he was surprised he had not thought of it at once.

The weapon was there at hand, in the secret cubby-hole in the bureau. He took it out and put three rounds in the cylinder. He hoped one would be enough, but he had to make certain; nothing must be left to chance.

Then he waited. It would have to be done after dark, but before his father and mother returned from Norwich. But he felt sure they would not be back until late in the evening. They would go to a cinema to finish off the day before setting out on the return journey. He would have ample time to do the deed and be back at Mill House before they arrived home.

During the waiting doubts began to creep in. Could he do it? Would he have the courage when it came to the point? But he only had to bring back into his mind the picture of what he had seen in the bedroom at the cottage to cause all the anger to come flooding in again with the conviction that the fiend Cooper must not be allowed to live. He had to be destroyed, once and for all.

Yet when he had come to this conclusion he thought of something else. Suppose Uncle Hector returned home before he could do the deed. Would he not hear the shot and come to see what was the reason for it? Perhaps. And Aunt Eva too. Well, he would have to make sure they were not there. This was one of the days when his uncle usually came home late and Aunt Eva would visit friends in the village, since she hated to spend evenings at home alone.

He could not count on any of this of course; so he would have to make sure there was no one in the cottage before he called on Cooper. If either of them was there he would have to postpone the killing to another time. It was an odd thing that when he had thought this out he felt a curious sense of relief that he might not after all have to deal with Cooper that day; for he knew in his heart that if the thing was not done then it never would be. So in a sense it would be fate that made the decision and not he. There was comfort in that reflection.

★　★　★

Time passed slowly. He heard the mill stop working and Jacob Ward walk past the front of the house on his way home. The other men had already gone, their day's work finished. Now he was really alone.

He felt hungry. He got himself some biscuits and a glass of lemonade; and after this simple meal he waited again, watching the clock, listening to the seconds ticking away.

In those last days of August dusk came early. He lighted no lamp in the house, but waited in the gathering darkness.

It was getting on for eight o'clock when he

left the house and walked the short distance down the road to his destination. The revolver was in his jacket pocket, and he could feel the weight of it dragging that side of his jacket down. It was cloudy but dry, and he met no one. As he came to Cooper's house he saw that a light was showing in one of the front windows, but in the cottage opposite all was dark; so it seemed that Uncle Hector had not yet returned from work and that Aunt Eva had gone out. He took this as a sign that fate had decided that Cooper must die and had chosen him as the instrument to carry out the deed. Now he could not draw back.

He went round to the back of Cooper's house and saw that the kitchen was lighted too. He hesitated on the doorstep, and he was trembling. He had come this far, but could he even now really go through with it? Why not run away now, before any harm was done? Wouldn't that be the sensible thing to do?

But he stayed there. He lifted his hand and rapped with his knuckles on the door. From then on it was as if it were all a dream in which every action was taken without any conscious thought, because that was the way it had to be. It was not he, Martin Gray, who was doing it but an automaton in his shape.

The door opened and Stanley Cooper stood there in shirt and trousers; the shirtsleeves rolled up to reveal hairy forearms, the trousers supported by braces. There was a lamp in the kitchen behind him that gave him a kind of halo.

'Why, hello, Sonny Boy,' he said; and he sounded surprised. 'What brings you here?'

'I've come to kill you,' Martin said.

He pulled the revolver out of his pocket, and his right hand was shaking so much that he had to use the other hand to steady it. He pointed the gun at Cooper's chest.

'Now why would you want to do that?' Cooper asked. He did not seem at all frightened. He seemed merely amused. 'Why me?'

'Because I saw you this afternoon with my Aunt Eva. In the bedroom in the cottage.'

This seemed to take Cooper somewhat aback. 'You were there?'

'Yes, I was there.'

'You didn't make much noise. I never heard you. Well, you're a one, you are. And now you're going to shoot me for the honour of your Auntie. Is that it?'

'Yes.'

'She isn't worth it, you know. Your dear Auntie Eva is no better than a bloody whore.'

Martin was not sure just what a whore was, but he guessed it was something bad, and it made him even more angry with Cooper.

He said: 'She is not. You're the whore.'

Cooper laughed at this, which was not a wise thing to do; not with a gun pointing at his chest, even if it was not being held very steady.

'Now look, Sonny Boy, why don't you go and play games with your toy gun somewhere else? You've had your joke, but don't overplay your hand.'

Martin was surprised that Cooper should think the revolver was a toy. But the light was poor and he might not have been seeing it very clearly. That was why he was not frightened.

'It's not a toy,' Martin said. 'It's a Colt thirty-eight.'

'Is it really now? A Colt thirty-eight. My, my!'

It was apparent that he did not believe a word of it. He took a step towards Martin, who was shaking; scared but still standing his ground.

'Stop!'

Cooper took another step and Martin pressed the trigger. He had to press it quite hard to work the double-action which brought the hammer back and then released it. And in the end the result was disappointing; it was nothing but a metallic click.

Cooper came to a halt and laughed again.

'You forgot to put the cap in. No bang, bang.'

Martin knew the real reason why there had been no bang; it was because the hammer had fallen on one of the empty chambers in the cylinder. Cooper's taunt incensed him. Now he really would show the man. He pressed the trigger again, and again there was a click but no bang.

Cooper said: 'That's enough. Your time's up, Sonny Boy. Do you go of your own accord or do I have to give you a kick up the arse?'

He started to advance again, and Martin was afraid of the man. He wanted to turn and run, because Cooper was so big and he was so small in comparison. But he did not run; it was as if his legs refused to move. Cooper's chest was almost touching the muzzle of the gun when he pressed the trigger for the third time.

There was no empty chamber waiting for the hammer to fall this time; there was a live cartridge, and the bang came sure enough. Martin was surprised by the kick of the gun in his hands; if he had been standing further away the bullet might have gone over the target as the barrel jumped. But he was too close for that; too close for any possibility of a miss.

He stepped quickly back, and Cooper just

collapsed in the doorway. In the end it had all been so easy; so very easy to kill a man.

There was something else he had to do. He knew it, but could not think for the moment what it was. And then he remembered: he had to get rid of the gun. He had already decided on the place: the cesspool behind Cooper's pigsties. It was dark there, but not too dark to make out the vague shape of the pool of stagnant sewage. He approached to within a foot or two of the brink and dropped the revolver in. It sank at once.

The ground near the cesspool was damp and rather muddy. He found a stick nearby and used it to obliterate his footmarks. There had been no rain for weeks, and elsewhere the ground was so hard and dry that his shoes made no mark.

He went back to Mill House and straight to bed. He was in bed when his parents arrived home, and he pretended to be asleep when his mother eame into his bedroom. But he had not slept. He simply could not face them now; they would have seen in his manner that something was wrong; he would not have been able to hide it. In the morning he would be better able to act as though everything were normal. And very soon that morning the body would have been found and nobody would be thinking of anything else.

★ ★ ★

It came as a shock to him when Uncle Hector was suspected of being the murderer. And then later he was arrested and charged with the crime. Somehow, this possibility had never entered his head. But it did not worry him. Knowing that his uncle was innocent, he imagined that in no way could he be convicted of a crime he had not committed. He had a touching belief in the infallibility of British justice and was convinced that no jury would ever bring in a verdict of guilty in this case.

Reasoning thus, he felt no compulsion to step forward and confess that it was he who had in reality shot Stanley Cooper. All would be bound to come right in the end. Had not fate decreed it?

Unfortunately, British justice turned out not to be infallible, and an innocent man could be sent to the gallows.

Hector Langdon was innocent of the crime of murder and yet was hanged.

28

So Long Ago

'And you told no one?' Crystal said when he had finished the story. 'You let Daddy be executed for something you did, and you didn't say a word?'

'Oh no,' Martin said. 'You mustn't think I'm as bad as that. Right up to the last minute I was just hoping there would be no need; that he would be found innocent and all would be fine. But when the verdict of guilty came in and he was sentenced to death I had to speak up. I had to tell someone it was I who killed Cooper.'

'So who did you tell?'

'My father and the police.'

'But nothing was done.'

'I know. They just wouldn't believe me. They thought I was making up the story to save Uncle Hector. And of course it was the last thing the police would want to believe, because they'd got their man and he'd been convicted. For them it was a closed case, and they weren't going to bring a twelve-year-old boy to court charged with a murder for which a man had already been tried and sentenced to death. They would have been laughed at. And of course there was no way I could prove at that stage I'd done the killing. In the early stages, before the revolver had been found, it might have been possible, because I could have told them where I'd dumped it. But later, no.'

'But why in the end did he confess to the crime? He knew he was innocent.'

'I've thought about that a lot,' Martin said, 'and my belief is he did it for me. He must have turned things over in his mind and come to the conclusion that if he didn't take the revolver from the bureau, there were only two other people who could have done it — my father and I. Apart from my mother of course, who could be ruled out. I'd say he ruled my father out too, and that just left me. He knew how I adored your mother, and he may have guessed I'd seen something going on between her and Cooper. This is all conjecture, but it seems possible. Anyway, we'll never know for sure now.'

'No, we won't.'

'There's another odd thing. What he gave as the reason for changing his plea: that he didn't want to go to his death with a lie on his lips. Which of course was the very thing he was doing. I have this feeling that it was a kind of message to me. A macabre sort of joke between the two of us. A way of telling me he knew what I'd done and he didn't hold it against me. At least, that's how I've figured it out. I could be wrong, of course.'

'No,' she said. 'I don't think you're wrong. That's the sort of man he was.'

'So now you know. So how do you feel about marrying a non-convicted murderer? Do you want to pull out now? There's still time.'

'Don't be an idiot,' she said. 'I love you, don't I? And it was all so long ago.'

'Well, I'm glad you feel that way. I knew I'd have to tell you sometime, but I never imagined it would be on Liverpool Street Station in the middle of the night.' He looked at his watch. 'It's past three o'clock. How would it be if we went back to the canteen and had an early breakfast? Then if it's a fine day we could have a snooze in Hyde Park or somewhere like that. We might even do a spot of you-know-what on the grass. I've heard it's done.'

'Not by me,' she said. 'There are some things I just will not do in public, and that's one of them. Besides, we might get arrested for committing an offence under the public order regulations or some such. You'll have to wait for the embarkation leave.'

272

'All right then. Let's go to the canteen and sample the haute cuisine. I hear they can work wonders with powdered egg, dried skimmed milk and soya flour.'

'Ugh! It sounds repulsive.'

'Well, there is a war on, you know.'

'Now where,' she said, 'have I heard that before?'

THE END

We do hope that you have enjoyed reading this large print book.

Did you know that all of our titles are available for purchase?

We publish a wide range of high quality large print books including:
Romances, Mysteries, Classics
General Fiction
Non Fiction and Westerns

Special interest titles available in large print are:
The Little Oxford Dictionary
Music Book
Song Book
Hymn Book
Service Book

Also available from us courtesy of Oxford University Press:
Young Readers' Dictionary
(large print edition)
Young Readers' Thesaurus
(large print edition)

For further information or a free brochure, please contact us at:
Ulverscroft Large Print Books Ltd.,
The Green, Bradgate Road, Anstey,
Leicester, LE7 7FU, England.
Tel: (00 44) **0116 236 4325**
Fax: (00 44) **0116 234 0205**

ρ